A Story of Love at First Sight

The Dancer

J. M. Dietz

WORD ASSOCIATION PUBLISHERS

www.wordassociation.com
1.800.827.7903
TARENTUM, PENNSYLVANIA

Printed in the United States of America.

ISBN: 978-1-63385-447-5

Published by
Word Association Publishers
205 Fifth Avenue
Tarentum, Pennsylvania 15084

www.wordassociation.com
1.800.827.7903

Publisher's Cataloging-in-Publication Data

Names: Dietz, J.M.
Title: The dancer : a story of love at first sight / J.M. Dietz
Description: Tarentum, PA : Word Association Publishers, 2022. | Includes bibliographic references. | Summary: An engineering student falls in love at first sight with a strip club exotic dancer in 1950s Pittsburgh. They part through a misunderstanding but later find a second chance for love.
Identifiers: ISBN 9781633854475 (pbk.)
Subjects: LCSH: Engineering students -- Fiction. | Man-woman relationships -- Fiction. | Stripteasers -- Fiction. | Pittsburgh (Pa.) -- Fiction. | BISAC: FICTION / Romance / General. | FICTION / Romance / Historical / 20th Century.
Classification: LCC PS3604.I38 D548 2022 | DDC 813 D54--dc23

*Dedicated to the memory of
My wife, DOLORES, the love of my life*

Other books by J. M. Dietz:

The Braska Boys

A Christmas in Pittsburgh

Background

S everal decades ago, before I was published, I wrote little stories. They were just for entertainment, read only by friends and relatives. My wife enjoyed them. She asked me to author a story just for her. She wanted it to be about love. I told her that I wrote children stories and mystery adventure tales.

She insisted. After many months, I wrote this. She liked it! She was the only one to read it. I thought it was lost. It was never seen again and was forgotten.

Recently, I found the only copy in the back of a file cabinet. What should I do with it? My wife would have said to put it into print and let everyone read it. (Did I mention, she was biased about my works?)

So, this is it. I hope you like it.

- J M DIETZ

CHAPTER 1

Martin

Looking out the window at the cold wintry scene far below him, Martin Malone felt depressed. Watching ice flowing down the Allegheny River to meet the dirty Monongahela River at the Point, forming the wide Ohio River seemed like his life. Flowing away, wasting time, going nowhere particular. In two days, I will be twenty-five, one third of my life gone at best, and nothing to show for it.

Sure, I have a decent job, good health and almost out of debt but something was missing. I have no future. After graduating from college with a BS in Engineering I then moved here to Pittsburgh. These last three years were a symbolic act of breaking the umbilical cord with my family back home. But I see no future here. With no close family and just three good friends, I feel depressed and lonely. It is like I am on one of those ice floes, just drifting with the current with no planned destination or defined route.

The dreary, dirty scene below made me feel worse, all in black and gray. In summer I used to enjoy this view. When the trees were blooming, the Fountain spouting sparkling waters high into the sky at the Point Park below, a multitude of colors arrayed in every open area, this view had exhilarated me. It gave me feelings of progress, energy, and hope. This feeling I have now is just getting old.

It's nearing 5 0'clock, the quitting time at PPG. The day had changed into a cold evening. Snowflakes were starting to fall.

My three friends, Ron, Bubba and Chuck bounded into my office like three teenagers, all excited about making plans for the evening. We discussed options and agreed to meet after work at a bar in the Strip District called Rosa's. We would start at Rosa's, have a few beers, a bite to eat and check out the usual flock of young and willing girls. We would each make our own way there in our own cars in case we got lucky.

Upon entering the crowded bar, we took a table for four. It happened to be near the Ladies Room which made checking out the girls easier since they all passed by, eventually and often stood, and chatted by the door while waiting to enter.

After eating some bar food and consuming many beers, I disclose, "In two days it will be my birthday and I can't shake this feeling of depression." The boys decide to throw a party for my birthday, details unknown, currently. I decide to leave early and go home to feel sorry for myself.

I had too many free beers that the boys were buying, in anticipation of my approaching birthday and was getting loaded. Besides, I was in no shape to meet and impress girls tonight. I had noticed this attractive girl when I first came in and when our eyes met, they locked on each other, and we just stared at each other. It became very intense and only stopped when a passersby stepped between us. When they had passed by, she was gone. After drinking all those beers, I was slow getting to my feet and when I did, she was lost in the crowd and then my attention wandered as they handed me another drink. Maybe I will see her next time.

After Marty leaves, Ron, Bubba and Chuck start to plan a surprise party for Martin. Unnoticed by them, two girls are standing nearby, waiting to enter the Ladies Room and who were able to overhear the conversion. These two girls mingle with the other waiting girls but linger to hear most of the details. Other females come near, waiting in line to enter the Ladies Room and these two prying girls had to move on. When they return, they believed that nothing was lost in those few absent minutes and stay till all plans were finished, then they return to their table.

The men discussed various plans and finally decide on renting a Private Party Room upstairs at Rosa's. After talking about getting four Hookers, a night's supply of alcohol and the cost of the room rent they decide on getting only one girl, just for Marty. Bubba said, " I heard about a girl, a professional, who does a Belly Dance then strips. I even have her business card in my wallet."

Bubba then goes to the phone, calls the girl's number, and makes all the arrangements. Chuck goes to Rosa's Manager and reserves the Private Party Room. Everything is set. Now only to convince Marty to accept his birthday gift. They forget the dancer's business card and leave it on the table.

The next day, at work, Ron, Bubba and Chuck find out more details about this Dancer/Stripper. She is also a Hooker but keeps that business apart from her agency. From friends they learn about the other services she will perform, for group sex or just with an individual, and the price structure for each sex act. They decided it would be too costly for her to have sex with all four of us and too costly to have her have sex with Martin while they all watched. We then decided to limit the party to Belly Dancing, then stripping and then sex but only with Martin. No others would be present.

Bubba leaves work and hurries to the booking agency and hires a girl for Friday night.

They then meet with Marty and tell the plan. "We will pay for just half."

I said, "You should have consulted me first."

They all respond, "It's already paid."

At lunch later that day they tell me about the party and the girl and say the cost of the party is on them, including the Belly Dance and the Striptease Act, but if I want sex with the dancer they will not pay and if you do not want this girl one of us would go in your place. " I finally consent but say, sex will only occur if she is exceptionally good looking. I never paid to have sex with a girl yet and do not intend to start now."

CHAPTER 2

I was looking forward to going to a single's bar after work. Rosa's up in the Strip District was more than just a single's bar, it had food, entertainment, and dancing. It was like an after-work nightclub. With no man in my life now and no prospects in this office building, a single's bar was my only option. I had not dated since Dec. and winter just is not the time to meet men. The few men I've meet in bars like Rosa's just were not my type, but hope is eternal. I will find myself a man one of these days. It has been a year and a half, since college, that I have been living by myself here in Pittsburgh. The prospects of finding the man of my life remained the same as always, poor. None of the men I had met caused that spark, that heart rush, which feeling of instant knowledge that he is the one, that I've read about. It probable is just all fiction. Although my mother insists that when you meet the right man, you will know. I just had to keep looking but I feel some of my best years are passing by.

At last, my melancholy reverie was broken by the entrance of my two best friends, Dolly and Janet. They were my age but, yet quite different. They were always smiling, laughing, and bubbling with life. They also always had a lot of male friends to choose from. That is what makes them so happy.

"Hey there Mary Bums, let us leave this old folk's home and meet some young strong men." said Dolly. "Maybe all three of us will get lucky tonight."

It seemed like all Dolly and Janet talked about was men. "I'll be ready in a minute."

We left the office and took the Shuttle Bus to the Strip District and got off near Rosa's. When we entered the dancehall the blast of noise and heat was a welcome sign. The walk from the shuttle stop was cruel in this late Winter weather. It was colder out than one would think, especially this close to the river.

Janet ran ahead to get a table while Dolly stopped a waiter to place our order. I went to the Ladies Room to fix my hair and face. When I returned, I neared a table occupied by four young men. All were good looking, but one caught my eye. Something clicked inside me. Could this be the one? Love at first sight? No, that is silly, but still he looked interesting. I slowed as I passed by and when he suddenly looked up, our eyes met. Neither of us looked away. I finally averted my eyes and walked away. My body got warm, and I felt myself flush. What a strange yet nice feeling.

When I finally got to the table, I excitedly said, " I saw the sexiest man sitting over there."

Janet said, "Where? Point him out."

"So, you finally found someone interesting Mary, it's about time." Dolly said, "Why don't you go over there and talk to him. Just lean over let him see some skin from your breasts and he will get interested in your return, that always works for me."

"That's something I couldn't get the nerve to do. Oh! He's looking this way now."

"Which one is he?"

"He is sitting at the table near the ladies' room, facing us. He is wearing a blue blazer."

"Well, if you won't go over there, we will. Come on Janet." Dolly said. grabbing Janet's hand. "We will bring him back for you."

I felt mortified. That is just the kind of thing they would do. They were both flirtatious and extremely cute. Getting men was never a problem for either of them. I could not do things like that. Even in high school or college I never made the first move. Normally not the second or third either. I have never dated anyone seriously or for long times. They just did not feel right to me. Oh! Lots were handsome enough, but nobody ever turned me on not even after passionate kisses. That is as far as my love life has progressed in my 23 years. Still a virgin and unwanted with no prospects in the future. In two more years, I will be twenty-five and I will the at the age my mother calls an unmarried girl, a spinster. Just the sound of that word made me feel depressed and yet desperate.

Glancing around I saw Dolly and Janet still by the ladies' room door standing there trying to look nonchalant but not being very successful, to even a casual observer. What were they doing? It looked like they were eavesdropping. At least they were not just barging in and dragging him back here. I might just not mine tonight.

I drank my drink and theirs too, then ordered another round. They were still standing there. It was so obvious. They must be embarrassed just standing there. There was a cluster of girls standing there now, waiting to go in. Maybe it was not so obvious.

Dolly and Janet laugh about the overheard plans and say what a good opportunity this would be to get Mary to meet her dreamboat. If only they could somehow substitute Mary for the dancer. They see the forgotten business card and pick it up. Then they go to tell Mary about the overheard plans.

"Mary, we have it all planned. They are going to hire a dancer for your dreamboat's birthday party. We will substitute you instead and that will be your way to meet him. There is only one small catch. Mary, you have to dress as a belly dancer."

When I hear their scheme, I was totally against this ruse. After much cajoling and a few more glasses of wine I agree to at least hear their plan.

If possible, I am to switch places with the dancer and preform the dance in costume. Then if I don't like the guy, I can just leave, but if I like him and the room and conditions are pleasant, I am to start a conversation. I am to tell him that this was my first time I have danced and ask how he liked it. Then the rest is to be up to me.

I agree to be near the party when it occurs and check out the situation. I will always be able to back out if I want to. I did not think there was any possibility of making a switch so I said, "OK, you can start to make plans, but it is not going to work." Never in all my life have I done anything like this and if I had not been drinking so much tonight, I would have vetoed this far fletched plan instantly. I could find other ways to meet that dreamy man.

The next afternoon Janet uses the business card and calls the dancer pretending to be the secretary of the one called Bubba and confirms the time and place. She also gets the girls name and the description and the cost for just the basic belly dance but was not aware of the availability of a strip or of any of the sex options. The dancer's business manager being careful not to mention anything over the phone to a stranger did not mention the stripping or the availability of sex for sale.

That night at Rosa's they all go upstairs and check out the private dining room and the nearby powder room. They believe a switch could be easily made but only with the full cooperation of the dancer. Dolly insisted that a switch could be made for a cash payment.

Janet suggests, "We will pay off the dancer Mary. It will not cost you a thing. Besides if you change your mind at the last minute, you can always back out. Come on, for once in your life take a chance. If you are really interested in meeting this guy, just go in shake your body a little, then sit down with him and start talking. What have you got to lose? If after meeting him, you don't like him just leave. Nobody will be the wiser."

I was starting to have all kinds of apprehension about going through with this ridiculous scheme, but their constant cajoling kept me from backing out just yet.

Their next step was to take me to the mall and visit the lingerie shop to find a belly dancer costume. With the cooperation of a salesperson, they decided on a transparent bra with transparent trousers. I insisted on using a bra and panties underneath but after much coaxing it was decided on using flesh-colored patsies and a black G string. They also purchased gold dancing slippers and a black veil.

We took the outfit over to Janet's apartment to practice a routine. I donned the complete costume and tried to dance seductively but just could not do it loose and free or with any sexy emotions. I just felt embarrassed and totally out of character. Dolly and Janet decided to start giving me drinks and to everybody's surprise I danced better and with a lot more sex appeal with every drink. They also gave me many suggestions on how they thought I should do the dance and how I needed to exaggerate my pelvic motions. No matter what I tried, I still felt foolish and was not planning to go through with the switch. Just to meet a man. I can always run into him again, somehow, somewhere.

They then decided that on the day of the party I would need a few drinks ahead of time to overcome my inhibitions and make this substitution believable.

Dolly and Janet decided that I would have to wear a lot more makeup that day and said they will do my makeup the night of the switch. They then took a few photos of me in a variety of silly poses saying they will be good for laughs later. When the roll of film was finished, I took the camera and withdrew the film. I said, "I'll keep the film. I do not want these pictures to be passed around the office."

I listened to all their talk and went along halfheartedly with their plans but deep down inside I felt I would never do this. The switch might never be possible, and I don't think I could ever dance in private in such a costume with a stranger watching. Anything could happen even though they would be across the hall, I would not feel safe. This whole plan would never come off and if it did, I am not sure that I would participate. To keep them happy, I just let the events flow and did not object too much and kept thinking about that dream of a man I will be able to meet.

CHAPTER 3

Martin

My birthday finally arrived. Little clusters of my fellow workers were spending the entire day discussing Marty and his stripper for the evening. They were betting I would not buy any of the sex options and if I did which ones.

Ron, Bubba and Chuck took me out for my birthday lunch, and we all had too many drinks. Back at work, I floated through the afternoon in a happy daze and started to dream of sexual fantasies.

At 5:00 o'clock we all drove to Rosa's to start the party. I hardly ate any of the happy hour food but started drinking an assortment of drinks. Finally, as seven o'clock was nearing, the boys took me to the private room and brought along a tray of drinks and some grapes. They even brought a spray can of whipping cream with many crude suggestions on how to use it. Ron, Bubba and Chuck went downstairs to meet the dancer at the door of Rosa's. When the dancer arrived, they immediately recognized her. She was about 5 feet 5 inches tall, slightly chubby, about 30 years old and looked a little haggard but was very well endowed. She carried a bag with her costume and a portable tape player. In their slightly drunken state, she looked attractive and very sexy. Bubba paid her for the belly dance and the strip and told her if any sex happened, she was to collect the money from Martin. They took her upstairs to the girl's room where she could change and showed her the room where Martin was waiting. Then they left to go downstairs to drink and laugh and dream wistfully about being in Marty's place.

CHAPTER 4

We three girls were waiting in the girl's room when the dancer entered, and we recognized her from the description given over the phone. Dolly and Janet clustered around her pleading their cause to replace her with me, the customer's girlfriend. The lie worked and she agreed to this switch. They finally settled on a price of $100 plus she would keep all the money already given to her for the dance. She merely had to sit with the two girls, have a few drinks and wait for Mary to return.

It was now up to me. Should I go through with this? The dancer did not appear to be afraid to dance before a stranger and had been doing that for some time. What can go wrong? I can leave whenever I want to. I finally find a man I want to meet, and this is a clever way to meet him. He will never know who I am if I decide to back out. I took a deep breath and said, "I will do it. I will do the dance."

The dancer looked over my costume and set it will do and showed me how to use the tape player. The girls helped in applying an excessive amount of makeup. I glanced in the mirror at my reflection. I resembled a garish clown. I adjusted my bra, donned my veil, and covered myself with a robe, then took a deep breath and left the room to a chorus of.

"Good luck Mary. Show him what you got."

"Mary, don't do anything I wouldn't do."

Along with other inane sayings, intended to bolster my courage. I quickly ran across the hall, knocked on the door and entered the dimly lit room and locked the door behind me. My knees were shaking as I wondered if this was worth all the trouble. Just to meet a good-looking man. I almost retreated to the girl's room, but I had enough drinks in me to bolster my courage, so I slowly turned and walked toward the center of the room.

Janet went downstairs and returned with enough drinks for the three to last for several hours. After a quick drink, the dancer told them that she was losing money, but was getting tired of selling herself for money to strangers. Dolly and Janet immediately asked, "What are you talking about?"

The dancer said, "I was engaged to do not only a belly dance and a striptease but that any sexual acts that the man wanted I would provide at the quoted prices, to be paid by the John at that time. I always insist on getting the cash up front."

Janet sobbed, "This was only to be a simple belly dance, not a strip."

Dolly said, "Not any sex for sale."

The dancer assured them that is what the John had wanted and paid for. Not only the belly dance but for a full striptease and was going to discuss any sex acts after the dance and stripping.

Dolly and Janet both rushed across the hall to the private dining room to stop Mary before she got into bad trouble, but the door was locked from the inside as per the plan. Knocking on the padded door was to no avail. The only sound they could hear was a faint sound of Arabic music. Flustered they returned to the powder room and the dancer and the drinks.

Janet said, "She said that she wanted to get to know him. She's going to find out now."

Dolly said, "Should we notify the management and get her out of there?"

"No! We will all get into trouble, maybe even get her arrested. Our best bet is to stay calm and be near in case she needs help."

Returning to listen at the door for a few more moments and upon hearing nothing but faint music they looked at each other, shrugged their shoulders and returned to the ladies' room smiling.

Dolly said, "We might as well get comfortable and finish those drinks. She might be in there a long time. I know I would."

"She might be in there a very long time." Janet chuckled. "I think she is still a virgin. Let us join that dancer before she drinks all the booze."

CHAPTER 5

Martin

I was reclining on the lounge drinking a glass of wine when a knock on the door came, and the door opened slowly. A young girl appeared, dressed in an Arabian outfit, covered by a long robe. Her clothes were almost invisible in the subdued light. As she glided near, I saw that her face was covered with a veil, but she was the most beautiful built girl I had ever seen. She started to operate the tape -player but I stopped her with a wave. "First why don't you have a glass of wine with me?" I spoke. She stopped, did not say anything, just nodded and gracefully reached for a glass and took a sip. She then started the music and slowly started to dance and gyrate. I could see a smile on her face behind the veil as her eyes never left my face as I smiled and clapped. She seems to respond favorably. Her dancing became more sexual if that were possible. I thought she was the ultimate performer, extremely sexy from what I have seen so far. I would pay to have sex with this girl.

After each song I offered her another glass of wine which she graciously accepted. She had to hold the veil aside while she sipped. Finally, I told her, "You might as well start your strip by taking off your veil. It is just getting in your way. I paid for a belly dance and a total striptease." She stopped suddenly, looked at me for a while then very gently removed her veil. She was absolutely the most stunningly beautiful girl I had ever seen.

The tape changed from the Arabic style tunes to the melody from the Stripper. The dancer hesitated, confused. She then smiled slightly and started to sway to the new rhythm. She turned her back toward me and reaching behind her back, very slowly removed her gauze type bra. She collapsed it in front of herself and slowly turned around. Her breasts were still covered by her hands and the gauze. She swayed to the beat of the music and stared at me with that strange teasing seductive smile. With one motion she threw the bra at me and raised her arms upward and slowly danced in circles. Her firm and upright breasts had small pasties covering her nipples. The effect was intoxicating.

I was getting very aroused and wished that I had not drank so much. Definitely I was going to pay to have sex with this woman. I hope I could perform at my best. I started to rise and go toward her but each time she would laugh and gently push me back onto the lounge. I then started a rhythmic clapping in sync with the music and her dancing and started saying, "Take it off. Take it off." She would look at me with that sweet yet knowing smile and undulate slowly, directly in front of my face. Then when I reached for her, she would back off. She was quite a professional tease. I could not wait to see her naked.

She backed further away stood sideways and rhythmically removed her gauze trousers held them in front of herself and walked toward me. As I again reached for her, all I grabbed were her sweet, scented pants. She laughed and started a faster dance with lots of spinning, just clad in her G string and pasties. Somehow, somewhere she had removed her slippers. She was a vision of beauty and yet lust. I wanted her more than I have ever wanted a woman or ever thought I could ever want woman.

The music stopped, then a sweet soft melody started. She seemed a little confused. I thought that it was a wrong tape but then I thought this is where all the clothes will come off and sex with her will begin. She was just standing still, but her body was swaying slowly to the melody. I couldn't wait any longer and said, "I thought the price I paid for was to see you naked, completely naked. I want to see all of you before we discuss any sex acts and their costs." She seemed to withdraw away from me slightly and stopped smiling. She waited a while, then spoke for the first time in slightly more than a whisper and said, "You will get what you paid for. Now what kind of sex do you want?"

I said, "For starters you can kiss me all over and then take me in your mouth. Then I want to kiss you all over and then we will have sex till I cannot move. Then we will start all over again. Now how much will this cost me?" I reached for my wallet and started to pull out large bills laying them on the floor in front of her and said, "Now come here and let me start to feel you."

She did not say anything, just watched as I started to remove my clothes. Before I could get naked, she went over to the tape player, stopped it, and returned to stand at arm's length away but directly in front of me. Slowly she removed one pastie, then the other. My eyes were riveted to her glorious large and hard nipples. Standing stiffly still in front of me, she quickly lowered her G-string and stepped out of it. She then raised her arms sideways and slowly turned around in a circle. She was a vision of loveliness. The most beautiful and desirable woman I had ever seen. She stopped and faced me as I was admiring her and getting extremely excited. I lifted my eyes from her body and looked at her face and saw tears running from her eyes. When she saw me staring at her face and tears, she took a step backwards. Seeing this, I rose and stepped toward her, reaching out to grab her. A strange look came upon her face, like hate or revulsion. She put her hand out to stop me and said in a slow angry voice, "Don't touch me. Don't you ever touch me."

I stood there dumbfounded. What had happened? Had I somehow done something wrong? I said, "Have I done something wrong? You are a whore and I have the money. Take the money and start doing your job." I stood unmoving as she reached for her robe and wrapping it around herself, picked up her slippers, bra, trousers, and G- string. Then taking the tape player, she quickly left the room while all I did was swear and curse her, humiliated and frustrated.

In a kind of daze or dream, I wondered about the room. I could still smell her sweet yet musky scent. I didn't do anything for a while, just sat there drinking and remembering her in every detail. When the last of the wine was consumed, I vowed to myself that I would see her again.

Leaving the room when finally dressed, I returned downstairs. I went over to the table were Ron, Bubba and Chuck were having a drunken party. When I appeared they all stopped drinking and started to ply me with questions.

"How was she?"

"Was she pretty enough?"

"Did you screw her?"

"Give us all the details."

I sat down and told them only a part of my sad frustrating tale. "She was the most beautiful girl, the sexiest girl, the most desirable girl that I have ever met. I screwed her in every position till I could not move then she got up on top of me and forced me to screw her again and again till I couldn't move. I had to beg her to stop." I lied.

Chuck then asks me, "What did she charge? You know we said we will pay half."

I looked at the three of them, took a drink and said, "The truth is, she didn't charge me anything extra." I then said, "I am very tired, and I am going home. Thanks for the birthday party. I'll see you Monday at work." I then turned and slowly left.

Driving home slowly and very carefully to not get stopped for any traffic violation and then a DUI citation. I reviewed the night. I just could not understand what went wrong. It started out to be such a memorable evening.

CHAPTER 6

I am extremely nervous as I approached the door. It feels as if I am naked in his transparent costume even if I do have a robe over myself. My nerves are on edge. I want to turn and run, yet I do feel a nervous and sexual arousal. Maybe it is just the tight G- string rubbing against me as I walked or the pasties glued to my nipples, turning them hard as they bounced with every step I took.

Taking a deep breath, I knocked and quickly opened the door and let myself in before I changed my mind. There he was, sprawled on a lounge, shirt half unbuttoned, hair disheveled, a semi drunk grin on his face, motioning to me to come in. He looked marvelous. He was so sexy, my heart started beating faster if that was possible as I neared the center of the room.

I took a glance around the room. It was empty except for the lounge and a table covered with wine bottles and glasses. There was an empty bottle on the carpeted floor. I took a deep breath and thought I can manage this. He is so intoxicated that he won't notice my amateurish attempts at belly dancing and my veil and makeup should prevent him from ever recognizing me later if we ever did meet again. Setting down the portable tape player, I turned it on and adjusted the volume. A sensual Arabic music started playing. I wished that I had time to listen to tape beforehand so I could be better prepared. I removed my robe and turned to face him.

He just stared at me, then said, "Why don't you have a glass wine with me first?" That would be just the thing to call my jitters. I nodded and stopped the tape and reached for the glass in his hand. Oh, if only this was for real and not this charade, I would be ecstatically happy. I returned the glass, still having said nothing, though my thoughts were racing. I look so foolish trying to sip a glass of wine under this veil. Should I say something or try to be mysterious and say nothing? Should I touch him? Oh, what do these real dancers do? I decided to say nothing at this time.

I restarted the tape and as the music played, I slowly swayed to the beat. There was a smile of approval on his face, so I swayed more. I begin gyrating my hips and slowly turned around. Our eyes were locked together. The dancing and his nearness were arousing me again. When each song ended, he again offered me a glass of wine. I accepted it every time but decided not to look foolish drinking under a veil and started to remove it when he said, "You might as well start your strip by taking off your veil as it is just getting in your way."

Suddenly I froze. Stripping? No way. That was not part of the plan or was it. Did my friends, my former best friends set me up? Now what am I going to do? I did not just want to run away after going to this much trouble just be with him, and I certainly was not going to strip. I quickly decided to go along with this charade if I could, then stop before I got into any trouble. After all, there wasn't much of me he hadn't see already. So, I slowly removed my veil and watched his face he looked hopelessly transfixed. I started to dance again and felt that I could control this situation.

Then the music changed and the melody from Gypsy came on, the stripper melody. I decided I might as well give him just a little show. I never felt this way before. Was it him or all the drinks I had? As I swayed to the tune, I turned my back and slowly removed my bra. After all, it was transparent anyway. When the bra came off, I placed it in front of my breasts and turned to face him. He seemed in a trance, just staring at me. So, I threw the bra in his face and raising my arms, danced in circles giving him the full view. The freedom from the bra, the pinching of the pasties or maybe the wine, something was causing me to feel such a strong sexual urge. I started to dance, using my hips and pelvis in what I thought were private sexual gestures.

He started clapping his hands and saying, "Take it off, take it off, take it all off." As I danced near to him, he would reach to touch me, but I would smile and just back away. Finally, I decided to remove my trousers. What kind of wanton woman was I turning into? I turned my back to him and slowly stepped out of the pants. I just noticed that I had lost my slippers somewhere. I held the gauze in front of me, turned around and walked toward him clad only in this G- string and two pasties. I had a feeling of power over him that I never had over anyone before, and I had extraordinarily strong sexual desires for him. He reached for me again, but I let him grab only my trousers. The music tempo speeded up and I danced faster and with more abandonment.

Then the music changed to a slow sensual melody.

What am I going to do now? I thought, as I stopped dancing and just swayed.

I was waiting for him to say something romantic or to call me to him, as I was ready to fling myself on top of him. He finally said, "I thought the price I paid was to see you completely naked? I want to see all of you before we discuss any sex acts and their costs."

What? I was shocked. He could have taken me before by just asking, but now he thinks I am a whore. This whole evening was just a waste of my efforts to get him to like me. They were just a farce. All he thinks of me is that I am just a whore. No longer had I any sexual desires. Only revulsion for myself and toward him. I spoke for the first time. My voice, just barely a whisper said, "You will get what you paid for." Then, still terribly angry but somehow also being a little curious, I ended in a whisper, "What kind of sex do you want?" hardly keeping my anger out of my voice.

He said, "For starters, you can kiss me all over and then take me in your mouth. Then I want to kiss you all over. Then we will have sex till I cannot move and then we will start all over again. Now what will this cost me?" He reached for his wallet and started to pull out large bills and spread them out on the floor. He then said, "Now come and let me feel you."

Instead, I went to the tape player and stopped it. I returned and stood directly in front of him, feeling very cool and partly able to control my disgust for myself and with him. I slowly removed one pastie then the other. The slight stings only increased my raising anger but made my nipples hard and large. I then lowered my G-string and stepped out of it. I raised my arms then turned in circles giving him a full view of myself. Letting him see what he could have had but could never buy. I stopped and faced him. The first man to ever see me naked and I don't even know his name. Why I did this, becoming naked? I will never know. To make him want me, someone he couldn't have, to get rid of my anger, my humiliation. To debase myself even further as punishment. I did not feel right being naked. It was just something I had to do, at that time, that place.

My attraction or lust for him was gone. Gone forever. I could not help it, but tears started to flow. The first man I wanted, really wanted sexually, and I let him see me naked, and it is all for nothing. I suddenly felt cold, foolish, and totally embarrassed. I had to get out of here. He was just standing there swearing and calling me vile names. He again reached for me, but I pushed him away. I said, "Don't touch me. Don't you ever touch me." I quickly donned my robe and picking up the tape player, G-string, and slippers, I fled the room without looking at him again.

I rushed to the girl's room and started to sob uncontrollably. Dolly and Janet tried to comfort me, but I just cried louder. The dancer tried to explain that the stripping was part of her act and she thought we all knew that the sex was just her part, and not done as a rule and not condoned by her agency. They kept asking, "What happened? Were you raped? How did you get naked?"

I wouldn't reply and just said, "Nothing happened. I just stripped and then left." Then I started to cry again.

The dancer took her things and left. Dolly and Janet helped me to get dressed and checked to see if the coast was clear, then took me home using the back doors.

At home, I assured them that I was going to be all right, that I just wanted to take a bath and be by myself. After they left, I took a long hot bath and gave myself a vigorous scrubbing. I then donned a pair of flannel pajamas and went to bed. I spent the long night thinking about that evening and what could have been and what never will be. I then cried myself to sleep.

CHAPTER 7

Martin

I thought about her all night long. Why had she left me with no explanation? Did I do or say something wrong or bad? Didn't she like me? I thought these kinds of girls were not particular and did not refuse any customers. What went wrong? I couldn't sleep but thought about her all night recalling the shape of her breasts and the size of her nipples the curve of her hips the swell of her belly and the curly hair covering her privates. It was driving me crazy.

I stayed home all weekend, not even answering the phone. By Sunday evening I was determined to see her again. After all, we had her phone number, and I could hire her again. I planned how the second meeting would go, no dancing, no music, just the two of us sitting down and talking. I will find out why she left and maybe then I could get her out of my mind

At work on Monday, after hours of good-natured kidding by half the office staff, I managed to get Ron, Bubba and Chuck alone and said, "I needed to meet this girl again." They laughed and said she must have been some kind of a good screw and asked me to describe her and events in great detail. I would not talk about her only insisting that they give me her card. They said they no longer had it, having lost it somewhere, but could get another one tomorrow. All they could remember was her name. It was "Selena". They again told me that they had never seen her before and just saw her briefly that night.

Tuesday finally came and Bubba came over and gave me a business card. He said it was an extra one he got from a friend. It read, EXOTIC DANCER for hire. Groups or private parties. With a phone number. No dancer's name. Bubba said, "Just call this number and ask for Selena."

Later at my desk I called the number and a raspy elderly voice answered. I said, "I would like to hire one of your dancers for a private party."

She replied, "Have you used our services before?"

"Yes," I said, "We had hired Selena last Friday. I would like to hire her again."

"But Sir," she said, "We don't have any dancers named Selena. Never had."

I explained we had hired a dancer to be at Rosa's on Friday evening and we were so pleased with her that we would like to hire her again.

She said, "Wait a minute while I check my records. Last Friday we sent a dancer named Aletia to Rosa's. Does that name sound familiar?"

"She never said her name. It is just that Selena was written on the card."

She laughed and said, "The girls change their names all the time. Was she about five foot five inches tall, dark hair cut just below her ears?"

"Yes," I replied.

"Well, I can't help you now because she took a two-week vacation. Can one of the other girls take her place?"

"No. No." I answered, "I will wait till as she returns. I want only her. I will call again in two weeks. Remember me, my name is Martin."

Later I told Ron, Bubba and Chuck I could not get hold of her and for all of us to forget her. I stayed by myself the next two weeks not going to Rosa's and not going drinking or eating lunch with my friends. The two weeks passed ever so slow. Finally, the second Monday arrived. I called the number again and the same raspy female voice answered. I said," This is Martin again. I spoke to you two weeks ago trying to hire a dancer named Aletia."

She laughed, "You really have the hots for her, don't you? Well, she is back and remembers the gig. Where do you want her to go?"

"Tonight, at 8:00 o'clock, at Rosa's, same room." I said.

During my lunch hour I went to Rosa's and reserved and paid for the private room. I could think of nothing else but Aletia. I did not get any work done. After work I went home, shaved, showered, and dressed in my best casual clothes. I decided to bring along a bottle of good wine, just in case.

I got to Rosa's early and waited anxiously for her entrance.

At a little after 8:00 o'clock there was a knock at the door and a stranger opened the door. "Who are you?" I sputtered.

This middle aged, slightly chubby woman said, "I am Aletia." She started to laugh and said, "I thought something like this was happening. She went on to explain how three girls paid her not to enter the room and dance, but just to sit in the girl's room with two of them while the pretty one, in costume took her place. She then told me how the girl returned, all mad and crying. So, she took her things and left the three there and went home. No, she does not know their names or how to contact them. She thought it was just a joke between friends."

I thanked her and paid for her time after declining to see her dance, and she left. I took my wine home, at a loss as what to do.

CHAPTER 8

T hinking about last night just made me feel worse and I started to have spells of crying. I hated myself for my actions last night. How could I have been so foolish? I am glad he was so drunk he could never recognize me if we ever met somehow, and I will never go back to that place again. I will never see him again. How crazy could I have been to do acts like that, in front of a stranger. Why I don't even know his name. In fact, I do not know anything at all about him except that he is a vulgar drunk. He is crude and a sex fiend. How could I ever imagine wanting a relationship with him?

Yet I could not blame him too much. After all, he was expecting a whore. He did not know it was just me, pretending.

This could be a good lesson for me. Do not change who I am. I will stay the same old Mary, quiet, restrained, a prude and a virgin. I will save myself for Mr. Right and never get into a situation like that again. Tears started to flow again, and I cried the rest of the day.

Monday I will get together with Dolly and Janet, and we will make plans. They will try to find out more about him. Where he works? Where he eats? Where he lives and everything else, they can learn. Then I will never go to any of those areas, so I will never have a chance to accidentally meet him. I never want to see him again.

Am I attracted to this man? No. No. No. I don't even know his name. Then the thought that would not go away kept repeating itself. Was I attracted to this man that I would do anything, changed my character, my morals, just to attract him? I finally cried myself to sleep.

At work that next Monday morning, I called Dolly and Janet to meet with me in the girl's room during the first coffee break. It was important. They came in with knowing smiles on their faces and we sat down in the corner like three Cold War spies. I said, "First let me tell you both the exact story of Friday night. I related the whole sordid tale, expecting to receive compassion and sympathy but all I got was smiles and giggles." Questions came like, "Did he touch you? Was he drunk? Was he too drunk to do anything? Could you see if he was getting aroused? What would you have done if he had not mentioned paying for sex?"

I answered saying, "No he wasn't too drunk. He never touched me. I could see he was very aroused. I do not know what I would have done."

"Now that you both know the whole story, I need your help".

"You want us to help you find him?" they squealed in unison. Both with big grins on their faces.

"Yes." I said, "But not for the reasons you think. I want to know all about him. Where he works, where he eats lunch, how he gets to work, where he lives, and what he does during his time off. I want this information to be able to avoid him for the rest of my life. I never even want to pass him on the street."

Both girls said they would help and get right on this mission this afternoon, but when they left the room, each wore a silly knowing grin.

CHAPTER 9

Martin

The next few weeks passed slowly. My work was performed as if I was in a semi-conscious blur. I caught myself always thinking of her, even during important meetings. My work must be suffering. I became very lethargic, wanting to do none of my old activities. Party drinking or just hanging out with my friends no longer appealed to me. It was as if I was coming down with a new flu virus.

I knew the cause. It was that girl. What was it about her that I couldn't get her out of my mind? Was it her beauty? I would have graded her a nine plus out of 10. Was it her body? It was an eight out of 10. Her legs? Just nine out of 10. Her walking? It was an eight out of 10 but could go higher if she wasn't barefoot. Her belly dancing? Just a 7. Her stripping? It was an 8 or 9 but it caused a 10 reaction in me. In summary, she was beautiful built, a good dancer and very sexy and the total package somehow graded out to be a 10. All I could ever want in a girl, except she was morally bad. A prostitute. This could never result into a relationship. I would be better off by just forgetting her completely.

Yet, I still had her in my thoughts. How long had she been doing this? How many men had paid to sleep with her? How had she started in that profession? Mostly I thought, will I ever see her again?

CHAPTER 10

I t had been five weeks since Dolly and Janet had undertaken their special assignment, as they like to call it. They had branched out to utilized most of the young single girls in our office. First, they concentrated on the nightspot, Rosa's. A description of all four men had been given to all the girls. They called themselves, "secret agents." Soon they spotted the three men but not the main man. After several days and evenings, the three men were identified. Their names were Ron, Bubba and Chuck. They all worked at the same location, the main headquarters of PPG at the downtown office. My secret agents never saw the main man. We all assumed that he worked with the other three at the same location. The girls were all getting a big kick out of this, and it became the sole topic of conversation in the ladies' room. They still thought this entire search was hilarious and none believed it was just so I could avoid him forever. Maybe I was starting not to believe also.

The special assignment leaders, that is, Dolly and Janet, then started a morning, noon and quitting time stake-out at the PPG office building. They arranged our office staff schedule to have different girls stationed at all entrances at all three times. They did a valiant effort in the cold damp spring weather.

They soon spotted him. We now knew his working hours and his lunch hour. Our teams were able to get close and gather more information. The first big news was his name. By being near him, they heard people addressing him as Martin.

The other news was odd. He did not eat with or go out in the evening with his other three friends. He ate by himself at various diners and never frequented the same place more than twice. They found where he parked his car, a two-year-old black Ford coupe. Nobody tried to follow him home.

Getting his full name was easy for my agents. They just casually asked any girl he happened to speak to, who he was. It worked like a charm. Could those old TV shows showing this method have been for real? His name was Martin Malone.

As they were zeroing in on him, things changed. His daily pattern altered. He started eating with his three friends and after work all four would go to various happy hour bars and dances at different single bars. But never at Rosa's. He was seen talking to and dancing with many girls and often leaving with them. It did not appear that he left with the same girl twice.

Now this changing character caused the special agents to reconsider about him. First most thought he looked like a man who was sad and listless. Possibly like a man who had just broken up a relationship. He looked quite lost, and they all thought romantically handsome. Now they all thought he was a cad and agree with me that I should do all I can to avoid him at all costs. They concluded the assignment with his advice. "Forget him." I silently agreed.

Two more weeks passed, and he was no longer always in my mind. I became more like my old self. Pleasant, cheerful, and chatty but still without a man in my life.

On a cold rainy Wednesday in spring, I decided to run some errands and then catch a quick lunch somewhere, instead of my usual snack in our company cafeteria. While doing my errands, in my short raincoat and umbrella, I got my legs and shoes wet. My hair was a mess. My makeup probably was a mess also. As I was running a little late, I decided to duck into a little diner and grab a quick coffee and a sandwich. I got my order at the counter and with my tray, packages, purse, and umbrella, went to sit at the corner table. Somebody bumped into me. Like a klutz, I dropped my packages and purse while almost spilling my tray on a couple at the next table. I sat down and before I could reach for my purse and packages this kind gentleman retrieved them and with a chuckle placed them on my table. He said, "I'm sorry I bumped you as I was trying to get to this table also and I wasn't paying attention."

I looked up and it was HIM. I could not speak. I tried to say thank you, but all I could do was just mumble. I felt myself blushing and my breathing was labored. He became genuinely concerned and asked if I was OK. By then, I regained some of my composure and was able to speak.

CHAPTER 11

Martin

Today I was late finishing a task at work and left for lunch a little later than normal. It was raining hard so I ran to a diner I knew I could get to without getting wet by going through a few adjacent buildings. The place was packed. The patrons seemed to be dawdling over coffees rather than facing the weather outside.

Placing my order at the counter, I glanced around and saw one remaining table in the rear. Upon getting my tray I tried to race a soggy old lady to that table but we both arrived at the same time. When she stopped to turn around, I was so surprised that she was a young and attractive. I unavoidably bumped her. She stumbled and while trying to balance her tray she dropped her packages all over the floor. She placed her tray on her table and started to get a cute blush over her face. Before she could move or speak, I retrieved her packages and placed them on the table.

Repressing a laugh, I apologized and said, "I was also trying for this table." She didn't speak, just mumbled something and her face got redder. I got concerned and asked, "Are you okay?"

She said, "Yes, don't bother. I just swallowed a bit of food. I am okay, thank you."

She looked so sweet, wet, and so helpless that I did something that is not characteristic of me. I imposed myself on her by asking to take a seat at her table. She didn't speak, just got a little redder. So, I very ungentlemanly placed my tray down, put on my most charming smile and sat down.

After a bite and a swallow of coffee, I decided to open the conversation. I blurted out, "Do you come here often?" How stupid. What an old dated pick-up line. Quickly I said, "Wait, that wasn't a pickup line. I just wanted to have some polite conversation." She smiled but did not say anything. Her face looked less flushed. So, I added, "I just meant, I've never seen you around here before."

Then she said, "I never came to this place before. It always looked too crowded at lunch. It's just that I was running late and with the rain and everything, it seemed like a dry warm haven. That is, before I was trampled trying to get this last table." She made the comment a joke by having a teasing smile on her face.

She looked more charming than before, and she seemed to be more relaxed. I took a quick look at her ring finger and felt relieved as I saw it was bare. So, I decided to shower her with more of my wit and charm. I said, "Haven't I seen you before?" Wow, what another clunker from the past. Why can't I think of any of my usual witty sayings? I quickly said, "No, that's not another line. I really meant it. You do look familiar."

She started to get flushed again, so I added, "Maybe you look different when you aren't so wet? No, that did not come out right. I mean you look good wet. I am sorry, what I mean is, you do resemble somebody I must have known. "

Chuckling she said, "I don't think we have ever bumped into each other before. I have to go back to work now." She started to rise and gather her belongings.

I couldn't let her leave without knowing more about her, so I said, "Let me help you. I will carry your packages then make sure that you can make it back. I'm responsible for any damages and I insist on helping." Before she could speak, I took both trays away and picked up her packages, took her by the arm and escorted her outside.

As she raised her umbrella, I asked, "Which way to your job?"

"I work a few blocks away, at ALCOA." she said.

So, taking her the arm and tucking my head under her small umbrella, I said, "Let's go." We strolled along the sidewalks like old friends, jumping puddles and laughing like schoolkids. The trip was over way too soon.

As we neared the entrance to her building, she smiled and said, "Thank you kind Sir. This is where I work. I appreciate your concern, but I am fine, and I can continue by myself."

I could not just let her leave. I didn't even know her name. "Look." I said, "In case you come down with any future ailments or if any packages are broken, I better take your name and phone number. I will call you tomorrow to check."

She said, "Just in case something is broken, here's my business card. And what is your name kind Sir?"

Handing her my business card I said, "My name is Martin, but my friends call me Marty." Looking at her card, I said, "Hello Mary. Very pleased to meet you."

She said, "Likewise." smiled and then turned and ran into the building.

CHAPTER 12

As I sat there looking up toward his face, all my supposed hate and disgust vanished. His face came so near as he spoke. He was even handsomer than I had remembered. I do not know what he said. I was still trying to get over this warm wonderful feeling that was pulsating through my entire body. He spoke again, "Are you alright?"

I finally regained my voice. I answered, "Yes. I must have swallowed a piece of food." How terribly stupid of me. What an unsophisticated statement. Saying I swallowed food. Why I hadn't even unwrapped my food. Couldn't I have said something more gracious.

He asked, "May I take this empty seat?" Again, I could not speak. I felt myself blushing. Why I am behaving like a teenager. Before I was able to think of some polite remark, he sat down. Just as if he belonged there. To cover my embarrassment, I started to eat my lunch, trying to be as neat and sophisticated as my fluttering heart would let me.

He said, "Do you come here often?"

I immediately felt better. He must be a little nervous also to use such a line. I think my blushing must have lessened and I felt a little calmer.

He added, "Wait that wasn't a pickup line. I just wanted to have a polite conversation."

I was feeling more at ease as he seemed to be nervous and not the cocksure man I still vividly remembered. Not knowing what to say, I just kept on nibbling on my food.

Slowly and calmly he then said, "I meant, I have never seen you around here before." Feeling assured that he did not remember me from that night. I relaxed, smiled and said, "I have never been to this place before. It always looked too crowded at lunch. It's just that I was running late and with the rain and everything it looked like a dry warm haven." Then I added with a grin, "That is, before I was trampled trying to get to this last table." He blushed at that. This conversation was improving. I believe I can enjoy talking to this perfectly gorgeous hunk as long as he never remembers.

Then my heart almost stopped as he said, "Haven't I seen you before. No that's not another line. I really mean that. You do look familiar." This is it. He is starting to remember me. Now I felt myself blushing again. I started to plan a fast exit but wait, he is shaking his head sideways. Maybe he doesn't remember?

He smiled and said, "Maybe you look different when you aren't so wet. No that did not come out right. I meant to say you look good wet. I am sorry, what I mean is you do resemble somebody I must have known."

He does not remember, good. I can relax more. Feeling happy again I said, with all the assurance at my command, "I don't think we have ever bumped into each other before. I must get back to work now." I then started to gather my purse and packages. Before I could rise, he said, "Let me help you. I will carry your packages and make sure you can make it back. I am responsible for any damages, and I insist on helping." He took both trays away, picked up all my packages, he took my arm and escorted me outside. It all happened so suddenly. I didn't have time to react, and I didn't want to resist. Outside I raised my umbrella and hesitated.

He said, "Which way to your job?"

"Two blocks away. I work at ALCOA."

He said, "Let's go." Then he took my arm, ducked his head deliciously close under the umbrella and propelled me along.

We strolled along like old friends. Laughing, jumping over puddles, perfectly at ease. I didn't want the walk to end. I wish I had worked further away. Too soon we came to the office lobby door. I did not want this happy meeting to just disappear but did not know what to do. He solved my fluttering heart by saying, "In case you come down with any future ailments or if any packages are damaged, I better take your name and phone number. I will call you tomorrow to check."

I felt so relieved. He wants to call me. That means he wants to see me again. I felt my heartbeat speed up and the warm glow went through my whole body again. "Here's my business card with my name and phone number, just in case something is damaged." I said with a smile. Then I added, "And what is your name kind sir?"

He handed me his business card and said, "My name is Martin, but my friends call me Marty." Then looking at my card he said very sweetly, "Hello Mary, very pleased to meet you."

When he spoke my name, I could have swooned. It felt right. For the first time anybody saying my name made it sound exactly right. I could have leaned toward him, flung my arms around him, and kissed him full on the lips. Instead, I only said, "Likewise." Then I turned and ran into the building before I really kissed him.

CHAPTER 13

Martin

Walking back to work after leaving Mary was like walking in a springtime garden. Everything seemed so bright, colorful, and happy. I forget that it was still a cold blustery wet day. I was happy, no, giddish would be better to describe by feelings. I was smiling and greeting every passerby. Not my normal sour outward disposition.

I bounced into my office, took off my wet overcoat and sat at my desk to recall every moment, word, scent, and image of that last hour. All thoughts of work were temporarily forgotten. After just a few minutes of this delightful mental bliss, I was rudely brought back to reality by the entrance of Ron, Bubba and Chuck. They were arguing, in a friendly manner, about the plans for this evening's party time and wanted my input.

After listening for a while, I said, "I don't think I'll go with you this evening. I have a few errands to run this evening. Besides, I just do not feel up to it tonight."

They all stopped talking and looked at me.

Ron said, "Look at that silly grin on his face."

"He must have found another girl." laughed Chuck. "Or maybe he finally found that stripper we all spent weeks looking for without results."

Bubba smirked and then added. "It is a girl, isn't it? A new one or return of an old one?"

Sitting back, I said nothing, just smiled with what I thought was my noncommittal smile.

They looked at me and started to laugh. "He's met another girl. It looks like another batch of puppy love."

"Here we go again. Marty's in love with some girl he just met. Tell us about her. Where did you meet? At another belly dance? Are you going to see this one again?"

I told them the highlights and showed them her card. I said, "I think I'll call her tomorrow morning. Ask if everything is okay and ask her out to lunch."

They just laughed at me even more. I did not care. Their kidding did not bother me. I was still in that strange happy mood. They left the room saying, "Mike finally found a way to keep track of his new girlfriends. He gets their card. See you tomorrow and we will tell you what you missed tonight."

I kept looking at her card. Mary Burns. Research Assistant. Room 1034. No home address. No other details.

I reluctantly went back to work but without my usual enthusiasm. I wanted it to be tomorrow so I could hear her voice again.

I thought of her all evening, like a lovesick schoolboy. While making my usual supper of TV dinners and salads, I cut my finger and later broke a dish. All of this was caused by my idle daydreaming. Was this the real thing? Real love at first sight, just like in romance novels or the movies. Or was it just some type of intense physical attraction. I didn't even see her body, but I did notice that her legs were great, and her hands and wrists were slender and graceful. Her face was very well formed and pretty and on and on. I kept those thoughts swirling in my mind all night. I slept fitfully. Would morning never come?

CHAPTER 14

I was late getting to my desk. Depositing my packages underneath, I sat down and dialed Dolly and Janet, telling them I had important news and to meet with me in the girl's room. I took my purse and motioned to my bewildered boss that I had to go.

When we were clustered on the couch in the corner I told them, "I met HIM."

"Who?" They both said in unison. "Who?"

"I bumped into him literally, at this restaurant, and we ate together. He actually walked me back here and we both were under the same umbrella."

"Who? Who?" they both said again.

"Why Martin of course. I am talking about Martin Malone. Here is his card that he gave to me. We just spent almost an hour together." I smiled and said, "He was genuinely nice. A gentleman, though he did knock me down. That is how we met. We both were trying to get the last table and he knocked me over. No not exactly, you know what I mean. Then he asked if he could sit at my table and when I was too dumbfounded to speak, he just sat down. Right across from me. We just ate and chatted but then we left together, and he walked me here. He asked for my name and phone number and said he might call tomorrow. Isn't that great?"

"Isn't this the man you said you never want to see again?" Dolly said. "The man you never wanted to meet again?"

Janet then asked, "Did he recognize you?"

"No, he didn't remember me, but he did say I looked familiar. Of course, I look different. The other night, with all that makeup on, and today I was wet and just had a little lipstick on. Then that night I don't think he was spending too much time looking at my face." I chuckled.

Then we all started to laugh. Dolly said, "I knew deep down that you wanted to see him again, didn't you?"

"Oh, maybe, but never under those circumstances again. Today we just sat down like two strangers meeting. It couldn't have happened any better." I sighed.

"This is only the third time that you have seen him, isn't it?" Janet said. "Do you still think he's so handsome and sexy?"

"This is the closest I've ever been to him and the only time we've talked. Yes, he is still very handsome and still sexy. Very sexy. He even smelled sexy when we were underneath the same umbrella." After we left the room, I got through the rest of the day in a blissful dream. Only interrupted by phone calls from either Dolly or Janet pretending to be Martin and then teasing me.

That night at home, I decided I could not take any chances with my appearance at work in case we would meet again. I meant to be ready and decked out in my finest yet demure clothes. I shave my legs and under my arms, pluck my eyebrows, and wash my hair. I set the alarm an hour early and went to sleep still happy but worried what if he does not call? I finally had a solution to it. I will just call him and make up a trivial lie about some slight damage to one of my packages. With that comforting thought, I drifted off to sleep.

I woke several times and tossed and turned. I was not rested at all when that darn alarm sounded. I shut it off and immediately found a warm comfortable spot and started to drift off to sleep when I suddenly remembered. I must get ready, for I might see him today.

I showered and put on my best and sexiest undergarments. Although I could not explain it to myself why, he was not going to see them, not today, but they just made me feel better. More assured of myself. I dressed and ate a quick breakfast, then took special attention in choosing my outfit. Not too bold but not demure either. Definitely not my normal work clothes. As I took one last look in the mirror before leaving, I thought, this is as good as it gets and if he does not like me in this outfit I am lost. As I closed the door, I started to worry. What if he doesn't call? Will all this be for nothing?

CHAPTER 15

Martin

The first thing I did at work in the morning was to devise a plan. A plan to make her like me and to overcome my bubbling yesterday. Last night, I had decided to send her flowers before I called. What kind? I had puzzled on this all morning. Roses! Roses it would be. But how many? A dozen would be too much yet a single bud just not the right touch. I finally decided on six roses, not long stems, but in a vase, and sent to her at her office. Now what color? Red seems wrong for a first approach. White was not correct either. I finally decided on six yellow roses. I ordered them from a florist a block away and dictated the note. It read; Sorry I bumped you but not sorry we met. Marty. The florist assured me they would be delivered before 10 AM.

I decided to wait another hour, to allow for mishaps and then call her. By 10:45, I could not wait any longer and called the number that I had already memorized.

The phone answered on the first ring. A pleasant voice said, "Good morning. This is Mary Burns. How can I help you?" She sounded different, yet familiar, with a pleasant sound.

I said, "Hello Mary, this is Martin Malone. How are you this morning?"

"I'm fine, thank you, and thank you for the beautiful flowers. They just arrived."

"I said that I would call to see if you weren't hurt and if I had damaged anything."

"No. I'm OK and nothing was damaged. Thank you."

"I feel as if I ruined your lunch yesterday. I would like to make it up to you by taking you out to lunch sometime. If that's OK with you?"

"It's not necessary, but we could meet and have lunch sometime. Why don't you call me sometime?"

I laughed and said, "It's sometime today and I'm calling you now. Will you have lunch with me today, please?"

"I just happened to have no plans for lunch today. Today will be fine."

"I'll wait for you in the lobby. I'll be there by 11:45, if that's all right?"

"Fine, I'll see you there. I have to go now. Bye." she said, and then hung up.

Before I could reply, the line was dead. The few seconds of talk kept repeating itself in my mind, repeatedly, and yet it seemed too short.

She did say the flowers were beautiful but used no other adjectives. Maybe she was just being polite and didn't really like them. Or else, she thought the message too forward. She did not mention the card.

It couldn't have been too bad. She agreed to see me for lunch. That is good. At least we can continue this relationship, if one can call this a relationship, on a more normal path.

Now to plan a luncheon location. It must be close to her building. I would not want her to walk too far in this weather. Taking a taxi would be out of place on a first date. Yes, I believe there will be more dates if I don't screw up this first one.

I finally decided on Valentino's. It was within a block. Quite pricey with a lot of space between tables, so we can talk privately. Not the kind of place a girl would go for lunch. It seemed perfect.

I called and was able to make reservations.

It was only then that I met with Ron, Bubba and Chuck and told him of the latest developments. When I told him about the roses and the card, they all started to laugh and make jokes.

"That's going to be a lot of trouble, just to get a date."

"Do you think a piece of ass is worth it? You aren't even sure you're going to get it."

"She must be some kind of a girl to get you moving in on her so fast. First it was the stripper and now it is some girl you just bumped into. You better get laid soon, so you can relax and go after girls with the same cool attitude that we have."

"Anymore, you get the hots for any good-looking girl you meet."

Finally, Chuck said, "I think we will go along and meet this girl. To see how hot she really is. She must be something to turn you on this way, or else you just need laid."

The others all agreed to go along with me, but I very strongly objected. I said, "If things progress as I hope, you will get a chance to meet her. But on my terms and at my choice of time."

Upon hearing that, they all left chuckling, saying they wanted to hear the details after lunch.

I combed my hair, adjusted my tie, donned my coat, and left to what I hoped would be a new phase in my life. I did not want to be late.

CHAPTER 16

I sat at my desk all morning, too afraid to leave in case the phone would ring. He did say he would call today. I have a feeling he will not forget; he is not that kind.

The hours dragged on and on. When I looked at the time, I was surprised to find only two hours had passed. Oh, it is going to be a long day. An exceptionally long day if he does not call soon.

When Janet and Dolly came by, they stopped and wondered why I was dolled up. Dolly said, "I notice you are wearing fishing clothes. The type to catch a man. If you don't land him dressed like that and you already tried naked, then you better give up."

Janet said, "Give her a chance. He will be sober this time and she has all the advantages now."

As we sat chatting, they tried to calm my nerves with idle talk, while I just sat there getting more nervous by the minute. When the phone rang, we all jumped. Picking up the phone I said in my sweetest voice, "Good morning. This is Mary Burns. How can I help you?" My heart sank when the office receptionist spoke, "Hello Mary. How are you today."

I wanted to cut the chitchat short and rudely said, "What do you want?"

"You sound a little depressed. I have a delivery at the front desk that might cheer you up. We will have a boy bring it to you immediately. Be happy, bye."

I told the girls that a delivery for me will be here soon. We all sat on the edge of our chairs, waiting, wondering. I was twisted my hanky hoping, for what I don't know, just not to be disappointed. A sigh of relief gushed from my lips as I saw a boy with a flower arrangement approach. My nervousness stopped as I said to myself, he didn't forget, he didn't forget. Before I could do anything, the girls had the flowers unwrapped and placed on my desk. There were six beautiful yellow rosebuds. Quickly my desk was surrounded by all my fellow office girls, who were oohing and aahing. They wanted to know who sent them and why.

I finally found the card and sat back to read it, while all the girls waited impatiently. When I read it; Sorry I bumped into you but not sorry we met. Marty . My heart skipped a beat. The card was taken from my grasp and passed around for all to read.

I was questioned with, "Who is this guy?"

"If you don't want him, I'll take him. Sight unseen."

"When can we meet him? When are you seeing him again?"

I silenced them all by saying, "I'm expecting his call now."

Suddenly the phone rang. All the girls quieted, to cluster near my phone. I picked up the receiver and said, "Good morning. This is Mary Burns. How can I help you?"

A voice I only slightly recognized said, "Hello Mary, this is Martin Malone. How are you this morning?"

"I am fine, thank you and thank you for the beautiful flowers. They just arrived."

"I said I will call to see if you weren't hurt and if I had damaged anything."

He sounded so sweet and concerned. I wish I had more privacy. I answered, "No, I'm OK and nothing was damaged thank you."

"I feel as if I ruined your lunch yesterday and I would like to make it up to you by taking you out to lunch."

Laughing, I said, "It's not necessary but we could meet and have lunch sometime. Why don't you call me someday?"

He replied, "It's someday today and I am calling you now. Will you have lunch with me today? Please."

I looked around at all the girls listening to only my half of the conversation, and said, "I just happened to have no plans for lunch today. Today will be fine." There were high fives and grins all around.

"I will wait for you in the lobby. I'll be there by 11:45, if that's all right?"

"Fine, I'll see you there. I have to go now. Bye." I had to cut the conversation short because of the chants in the background.

"Mary got a boyfriend. Mary got a boyfriend." And all the good-natured laughter.

I wish that I had been more pleasant and chatted more. That is hard to do in the middle of a crowd. I will try to improve my social skills at lunch. Smile more and listen to all his words. That is what my mother always said when I was younger and going out on my first dates.

CHAPTER 17

Martin

When I arrived at the lobby, the lunchtime exodus had begun. The multiple massive lobbies were awash with people. People were going in all directions, into the building as well as out. Why wasn't I more specific as to an exact location? Girls were everywhere, standing, walking, or just clustered in small groups talking. There were many girls Mary's height and shape and I almost approached several of them. I could not find her, and our meeting time was past. This was giving me an uneasy feeling. Like I had lost her before we had a chance to know each other.

Suddenly I heard a voice behind me say, "Hello Martin. I'm over here."

I quickly turned and saw a vision. It was Mary, but she did not look like she did yesterday. She was beautiful. Radiant better describes this girl standing before me. She was standing there with a happy smile. Her hair wavy and shiny. Dressed in a two-piece blue suit with a frilly white blouse showing. She wore a gold pin fastened to her suit and was wearing gold earrings. Without a doubt, she was the most gorgeous girl in the lobby, if not in all of Pittsburgh. But the best thing about her was, she seemed pleased to meet me.

"Hello Mary," I said, as I rushed over to stand by her side. "I didn't know that there would be so many people here at this time. I was afraid I couldn't find you."

She just smiled and said, "You're taller and it was easy for me to see you. I'm glad we got together. Now did you mention something about lunch?"

I saw her mischievous smile and I relaxed and grinned back at her. Our luncheon date had momentarily slipped my mind. "We have reservations for lunch in ten minutes. I must apologize for staring, but do you look different today. Not as I remember from yesterday. You look great."

Taking her lightweight coat, I helped her get into it. A whiff of her sweet perfume caused me to almost miss her sleeves. I slipped my hand under her arm and escorted her out of the lobby and down the sidewalk. It felt natural, as if we had walked like this many times before. She did not pull away. In fact, it felt as if her arm was squeezing my hand.

"I made reservations at Valentino's if that's all right. It is just a block away."

"That's fine. I've never eaten there before."

It seemed like only minutes had passed but suddenly we were at the door. I helped her out of her coat and then removed mine and gave them to the checkroom girl. The Maître de showed us to our table, presented our menus, then left.

Holding her chair as she sat, I admired the soft lines of her neck and the curve of her back. Uncertain of how to act, I asked, "Would you like a drink first? Maybe a glass of wine?"

"I don't drink at lunchtime usually. It is a bad habit to get into if you have to work all afternoon. Today, I want to make an exception. I'll have a glass of white wine but only if you have something also."

"I feel like having a glass of wine also. It is like a happy occasion. I didn't harm you yesterday and nothing was damaged. Let us forget about the reasons why we are here. I'm glad we're together now."

We ordered our drinks and when they came, I made a toast. "May this be of the beginning of a beautiful friendship."

She smiled and said, "I'll drink to that." When the waiter returned, she ordered a cup of soup and a salad. I ordered soup and the veal special. After he left there was an awkward silence which I hurried to fill.

I asked, "Are you from the city. You don't sound like it?"

"No, not originally. I was born in a tiny town in West Virginia. I went to college here at Chatham then stayed when I obtained this job. It is a nice city. It still has a lot of the small-town atmosphere. Are you from this area?"

"Yes. I grew up in the suburbs. Went to college here also, at Pitt. Then stayed on. I interviewed at various locations, but Pittsburgh was as good or better than the others. Besides, I get to go home and get free meals from my mom whenever I want." I smiled at that inside to my history, then added, "With both of us living in the city for so many years, it's a wonder we never met before."

"Oh. it's still a big city. It's spread out into a lot of small communities." she added, with a blush appearing on her face. "We could have passed each other many times without remembering."

"No, that's not possible. If we had ever met before yesterday, I would have remembered."

I thought there is no way I could have met this lovely woman, even passing by, and not have been struck by her beauty and charm. Not remember her. That is impossible. There is something about this beautiful girl that was strangely familiar. Maybe she is the girl in my dreams? No, they were all different. None looked like her.

When the meal was over, she declined dessert and just had hot tea. I could have lingered over a desert but then only ordered coffee This pleasant hour, filled with pleasant chitchat was nearing the end. How should I ask for another date? I don't think she agreed to this lunch, just because she really thought I was interested in whether or not I had hurt her yesterday. No, she could have said that over the phone. She must have wanted to come with me today.

After I paid the bill and as we were leaving, I summoned all my courage and said, "I enjoyed this lunch with you. We seem to talk like old friends and that made the time go by too fast for me. I would like to see you again. A movie or dinner or both if that's okay with you?"

She looked up at me, smiled, and said, "That would be nice. I had an enjoyable time today. Call me sometime."

"I only have your office number. Do you have a home number?"

"Yes, but it is in the phonebook also, under just my initial. Do you still have my card?"

Retrieving her card from my wallet, I wrote her home number down, along with her address. My spirit was singing inside. She wants to see me again. Great! I blurted out, "Are you free tomorrow evening?"

"Yes I am." she laughed. "Tomorrow is fine."

We reached the entrance to her building. What do I do now? What I wanted to do, was to hold her in my arms, cover her lips with kisses, and never let her go. How would she react to that? Probably slap me and never see me again. Should I just shake hands? But my palms are wet from nervousness. She would notice that.

At the doors, she stepped aside, turned to me, and said, "I had a wonderful time Martin, but I must get back to work now." She proffered her hand and smiled sweetly.

I took her hand in both of mine. Held it for a second, then said, "I can't wait to see you again. Tomorrow is such a long time away. I'll call you tonight."

With a smile, she turned to enter the building, then looked back, and gave me a slight wave goodbye. I waved back but it was too late. She had turned and soon disappeared. I stayed, hoping to get one more glance at her, but to no avail. She was gone. I was overcome with such a strange feeling of loneliness, it dampened by previous high spirits.

Returning to work, I tried to recall her every word, every gesture, every expression. Just to recall any of them, I thought, that would suffice till I saw her again.

CHAPTER 18

J ust before I was to leave to meet Martin, I entered the ladies' room for a final checkup. Several of my friends were also there, to give advice, encouragement, and tips on grooming aids. I didn't need any of this attention but suffered through it with a good-hearted grin. They all meant well. It is just that I am treated like their little sister. Most are only a few years older, and even the girls my age, like Dolly and Janet, treat me like a mere child. Is it so obvious that I lack experience? I have had dates before, lots, but nothing serious. Nothing lasting. Maybe I do need help this time?

The girls from the office escorted me to the elevator, and down to the lobby, with giggles and crude jokes. I pleaded, "Please leave me alone. I do not need you. I can manage this myself."

Janet said, "We won't bother you. We just want to watch."

When the elevator reached the lobby, we all exited, and the girls dispersed, to watch nonchalantly from various sections of the lobby. It looked like I was the First Lady and was guarded by a smiling contingent of Secret Service Women.

Looking around I could not see Martin. Oh. We never specified which lobby. I hurried to the door where we parted yesterday. There he was. His back toward me, standing so tall and straight. I stopped for a moment, just to admire him. He was turning his head, trying to find me, and appeared to be a little frantic. Good. He misses me.

Walking up close behind him, I said, "Hello Martin. I'm over here."

He quickly turned, and a kind of dazed smile appeared on his handsome face. He did not speak for a moment, then said, "Hello Mary."

Quickly he rushed to stand by my side. "I didn't know that there would be so many people here at this time. I was afraid I couldn't find you."

Glancing around, all l saw were the office girls, looking smug, and starting to inch closer. We have to get out of here and get some privacy. "You're taller and it was easier for me to see you. I am glad we got together. Now, did you mention something about lunch?" I smiled to make that last line a joke.

"We have reservations for lunch in 10 minutes. I must apologize for staring, but you look different today. Not as I remembered from yesterday. You look great."

I just smiled, thinking of all the time and effort it took to get this look. It was worth it to get such a reaction from him.

He took my coat and held it for my arms, and gently placed it around my shoulders. It was so natural and yet so intimate. Placing his hand on my arm, he escorted me from the building.

The feeling was so great that I squeezed his hand ever so gently as we walked away. From the corner of my eyes, I saw the office girls, all nodding and smiling.

"I made reservations at Valentino's if that's all right with you. it's just a block away."

"That's fine. I've never eaten there before." I had heard about it from some of the girls. Expensive. Quiet and spacious. Yet private. Supposed to be for lovers.

When we entered, he took my coat and checked it with his. He had his hand on my elbow as we were led to our table, then held a chair as I sat down. He was a perfect gentleman. I acknowledge by saying, "Thank you."

"Would you like a drink first?" he said." Maybe a glass of wine?"

What should I say? Now, I do not want him to think I'm a prude and I don't want him to think I normally have a drink at lunch. Oh well, I could use a drink right now to relax myself. "I don't drink at lunch usually. It is a bad habit to get into if you have to work all afternoon. Today I want to make an exception. I will have a glass of white wine, but only if you have something also."

"I feel like having a wine too. It is like a happy occasion. I didn't harm you yesterday and nothing was damaged. Let us forget about the reasons why we are here. I'm only glad we're together now."

When I heard that, I felt a blush starting. I was getting giddy again. What do I say after that? Thankfully, the drinks came. I raised my glass, but before I could take a sip, he looked into my eyes and said, "May this be the beginning of a beautiful friendship."

Another warm feeling pulsed through my body. I could hardly keep from reaching over and grasping his hand. I did not want to speak just then. My lips were trembling so badly, but I took a breath and said, "I'll drink to that." What a shallow reply. Why couldn't I say something witty or at least more sophisticated.

When the waiter returned, I was starved, but I stopped myself in time and just ordered a cup of soup and a salad. I did not want him to think I ate like a pig.

"I'll have a cup of soup and the veal special." he said.

When the waiter left, he said, "Are you from the city? You don't sound like it."

Taking another sip of wine, I relaxed, and said, "No. Not originally. I was born in West Virginia. I went to Chatham College and stayed on when I graduated when I got this job. It is a nice city. It still has a lot of small-town atmospheres. Are you from this area?"

"Yes. I grew up in the suburbs. Went to college here also, at Pitt, then stayed on. I interviewed at various locations, but Pittsburgh was as good or better than the others. Besides, I get to go home and get free meals from my mom whenever I want."

I am so glad he decided to stay. He is friendly with his mother too. He came from a nice family.

Looking at me, he said, "With both of us living in the city for so many years, it's a wonder we never met before."

My gosh. Is he beginning to remember that night? Did he always remember and is faking this whole thing? No. He must be sincere. Taking a deep breath, I replied, "Oh, it's still a big city. It is spread out into a lot of small communities. We could have passed each other many times without remembering." I felt a blush go to my face as I remembered that night.

"No. That's not possible. If we had ever met before yesterday, I would have remembered."

Then it is for real. He doesn't remember that night. He is not doing this in some nefarious way to even the score. He must like me or starting to like me, just for myself. I started to get warm again and felt another blush coming. Thank God the waiter came with our food.

Eating the food slowly, I tried to eat ladylike. Small bites and delicate chewing. I remembered that I had eaten only sparsely since lunch yesterday. Too busy planning for this luncheon to think about food. When finished, I was still hungry but declined any desert and ordered only hot tea.

After a pleasant yet too brief time, lunch was over. We left the restaurant, walking closely together. He said, "I enjoyed this lunch with you. We seem to talk like old friends and that made the time go fast, too fast for me. I like to see you again. A movie or a dinner or both if that is okay with you?"

Yes! Yes! I wanted to scream. I controlled my features and voice and said, "That would be nice. I had an enjoyable time today. Call me sometime."

"Are you free tomorrow evening?"

Feeling so relieved and happy, I replied, "Yes I am. Tomorrow is fine." Did I answer too fast? Did I appear too eager? If so, too bad. I want him to know a little how I feel.

We reached the entrance to my building. I glanced around and saw Dolly and Janet standing just inside the doors, trying to look inconspicuous. Ignoring them, I thought what should I do now? Offer my hand in a business type shake or lean toward him and kiss his cheek, and say thanks for lunch?

Deciding on a friendly handshake, I put up my hand and said, "I had a wonderful time Martin, but I must get back to work now."

He took my hand in both of his, squeezing it slightly, and said, "I can't wait till I see you again. Tomorrow is such a long time away. I'll call you tonight."

With that thought on my mind, I entered the building, turned to him and waved goodbye.

CHAPTER 19

Martin

I attacked my work all afternoon, making up for my inactivity the last days. Greeting everybody with a smile and a cheery hello, I felt that everything was OK with the world. Especially my little world. Though I thought of Mary all afternoon, I was able to complete my work in a timely fashion and even do work ahead of schedule.

The time passed rapidly. Soon quitting time would come and then I could go home and place that important call to her. This would be our first real phone conversation. Sure, it was to confirm the details of tomorrow's date, but more important, it was that intimate chatting that would be a part of it.

Running into Chuck, Ron, and Bubba, just before quitting time, I briefed them on the details of the luncheon. I told them of my date with Mary for tomorrow night. They laughed and kidded me. They realized how serious I was getting about this girl. They decided that if I was serious and romantic about this girl, whom they haven't met yet, I should take her to Pittsburgh's most romantic location. I should go high on top of Mount Washington, overlooking the Three Rivers and the Point. I decided that was a good plan, thanked them, and said goodbye.

We would get together tomorrow morning to review my phone call and plans.

On the way home, I stopped at a car wash and had a complete service. Wash, wax, and interior cleaned. No spot of dirt or grease was going to bother my Mary tomorrow.

My Mary. Was I starting to think of her as mine? I mulled that around in my mind as I drove home, and the thought was giving me pleasure.

My meal as usual, consisted of frozen soup, a gift from my mother, and a TV dinner, that I could cook in the microwave, along with a salad. Desert was a piece of fruit. Cleaning up took only minutes.

What time should I call her? It was only 6:30 now. It's too soon to call. She might not be home yet, or busy eating. I'll wait till later. What if she needs to prepare for our date? She would need time to do things. What things? I don't know, but girls always need time before hand, I heard. I decided at 8:00 o'clock, not too early, and yet not too late. It was an awfully long time, till eight, as I just sat on the couch and watched the clock slowly past the time.

I called her number, as eight o'clock chimed. She answered on the first ring. "Hello."

"Hello Mary, it's Martin. I hope I didn't bother you."

"Hello Martin. You did not bother me. I was just wondering when you would call."

Good, she didn't forget, and she seemed pleased to hear from me. "I had a wonderful time with you today. The only problem was the time passed too soon. Is there anything you would like to do tomorrow evening? Anything, anything at all."

"Why don't you decide, Martin. I'll leave all the arrangements to you."

"Okay. Then I will pick you up at your place at 6:00 o'clock. We will have dinner on Mount Washington and then check out the shows in Station Square. How does that sound?" I caught myself holding my breath, waiting for her answer. Was it too much for a first date?

"That sounds lovely Martin. That is a great plan for the evening. That would be rushing me a little bit. I have to take the bus home and they are never on schedule. Why don't you make it 6:30?"

Good, she sounds pleased. "I have your address and you said it's an apartment building. What is your apartment number?"

She gave me directions to her apartment. In that part of town, I was vaguely familiar with the streets and anticipated no problems finding her tomorrow.

"My number is 324. But you must press the call button. Then I can buzz the door open."

"I'm glad you have some kind of security. I will have reservations for seven-thirty, and after dinner we can watch a show or something. If that's all right with you?"

"That's fine, but let's not make plans for anything definite after dinner until after we eat."

There started to be an awkward period of silence. What should I do next? We don't know enough about each other to just have a nice friendly chat. What to do? What to say?

I finally said, "It's like I've known you for a while, and yet, I don't know anything about you personally. I know I like talking to you and yet we are still practically strangers. If you are not busy now, let's play a game."

CHAPTER 20

After leaving Martin, I wanted to turn around and watch him walk away, but I forced myself to walk straight to the elevator entry. I was not surprised as Janet and Dolly followed just before the door closed. We rode up to our floor without speaking a word in the crowded cab but did exchange grins.

Taking off our coats, we agreed to meet immediately in our second office, the girls room. I saw my supervisor looking at me and I told her I would be back soon. She just smiled and waved me on.

Sitting on the sofa, I related the entire lunch in detail. This time the girls were silent. Intensely listening, looking dreamy eyed. When I came to the part about kissing or just offering my hand, they both spoke up.

"You should have kissed him."

Dolly said, "At least a little peck on the cheek, or brush up close and give him a small hug."

Janet said, "Seriously, what you did was right."

"Even though I wanted to do those other things, it was right, because he asked me out on a real date, for tomorrow night. He's going to call me this evening." I sat back and smiled at the two wide eyed faces.

"That's fast, Mary. That will be three days in a row with him." Janet said.

Dolly added, "Maybe there's something to not crawling all over a man on the first date, as we do. That just leads to quick sex, and then they find some excuse to break it off. Mary, I hope you find something that lasts."

"I hope so too. He is so sweet, and such a gentleman. Good looking too. He is a totally different person from the man I met that first night. I still find it hard to believe that he is the type that would pay a dancer to have sex with him. I know he was drunk that night. I also know my dancing and stripping aroused him, but I wondered was it me. Would any girl have pleased him just as well?"

Dolly spoke up. "Let's arrange another private dance, and this time I'll be the dancer. I'll find out if it's you or any good-looking naked woman that turns him on."

"Oh no you don't. I do not want you or Janet or any other woman near him, especially naked. He is mine. I found him and I'm keeping him to myself."

With that thought, we left and went back to work. I do not consciously remember doing any work. All I remember doing that day was dreaming about him. No not about him, but about us. I thought about us in various scenarios, what I would do and say, and what he would do and say. Some of the thoughts got to be very erotic, but most were just extremely warm and sensual. Riding the bus after work, I was still in a state of bliss. Only when I got off at my apartment house did I remember, I should have gotten off at the grocers a few blocks earlier. I did not want to go back, so I entered my building and decided to just eat a pizza tonight. I did not want to be away in case he called early.

My nerves were on edge by 7:00 o'clock. No phone calls, just my mother, and I felt bad cutting the conversation short, with an excuse and a promise to call back later. Why didn't he say when he will call?

I was starting to tear up and I was extremely nervous when the phone rang. I picked it up before it finished ringing, and said in my suddenly calm voice, "Hello."

"Hello Mary, this is Martin. I hope I didn't bother you."

Bother me? No, it is no bother. It just saved my life I thought. My whole body relaxed, and I got that warm feeling all over myself again. I answered, "Hello Martin. No, you did not bother me. I was just wondering when you would call."

"I had a grand time today with you. The only problem was that time passed too soon. Is there anything you would like to do tomorrow evening? Anything, anything at all."

I am glad he had an enjoyable time. I did too, but I didn't mention that. I just replied, "Why don't you decide Martin. I will leave all the arrangements up to you."

"I would like to take you out to dinner tomorrow. If I pick you up at your place tomorrow evening, say about 6:00 o'clock, would that be too early?"

"That would be rushing me a little bit. I have to take the bus home and they are never on schedule. Why don't we make it 6:30?"

"6:30 it is then, Mary. I have your address and you said it is an apartment building. What is your apartment number?"

"It is 324, but you must press the call buttons in the lobby, to let me buzz the door open."

"I'm glad you have some kind of security. I'll have reservations for seven-thirty and after dinner we can watch a show or something, if that's all right with you."

"That's fine, but let's not plan anything definite after dinner, until after we eat." There was a moment of silence. I didn't know what to say to break this spell. I knew what I wanted to say, like I couldn't wait. Or can't you come over now. But I just waited.

He finally spoke, "It is like I've known you for a while and it I don't know anything about you personally. I know I like talking to you and yet we are still practically strangers. If you aren't busy now, let's play a game?"

"A game? What kind of game, Martin?"

"Let me ask you a few questions and then if you want, you can ask me anything you want. How does that sound?"

I laughed and added, "OK, but nothing too personal. Now, me first. What's your full name?"

"Martin John Malone."

"That wasn't hard."

"No."

"It's still my turn. Where did you grow up?"

"I grew up in a small town, up the Allegheny River, called Kittanning, it's an old Indian name. I left home to go to college, but I went back every weekend. After graduation. I moved to the suburbs, then took the job I'm doing now."

"What's your family like? Do you have any siblings?"

"My father works in a glass plant. My mother is a homemaker, but she does a lot of social work. I have a younger sister, Susie, she is a senior in high school. I have a brother, Jimmy, who is a sophomore at Penn State. Now it's my turn Mary. What's your full name?"

"It's Mary Agnes Burns. Don't you ever tell anyone my middle name. I am thinking of changing it. It is so old fashioned. Very few people know my middle name. I usually just use any initial."

"Mary Agnes. That is nice, not old fashion at all. Where did you grow up?"

"I grew up in Charleston, WV. Went to all my schools there. I left to come to Pittsburgh to attend Chatham college. After graduation, the best job offers were in Pittsburgh, so I stayed in town. I took an apartment near my old school."

"Tell me about your family."

"My father works in a chemical plant. My mother is a homemaker, but she was a schoolteacher. I have an older sister, Peggy. She is married but is having some problems with her husband right now. Then there is the twins, Kate and Kathy. They are just fifteen. All my sisters are living at home now." I didn't mention that my sister, Peggy, is pregnant and that her husband, John, is in the Navy and insists on taking special assignments around the world. Leaving Peggy alone at some faraway Navy port. After a big fight, she left him to come home to have the baby, near her family. That kind of bad gossip is best left unsaid.

"What do you do in the evenings, when not talking to me?"

"Nothing special. What every girl does. I fix myself something to eat. Do the dishes, clean the house, and do laundry once a week. All the usual mundane chores. Then I go out with my friends a few times a week."

"Where do you go with your friends when you go out?'

"Oh, nowhere in particular. Movies occasionally. We frequent some of the single bars, no place special, to be truthful."

"You're not dating anyone now, are you?"

"No, not now. It's my turn to ask the questions." I wanted to change the subject away from my dating habits or lack of dating habits. "What do you do after work?"

"After work, my three friends and myself usually go to some bar, to wait out the traffic jams. We pick a place where we could get something to eat along with our drinks. After a few hours, we split up and all go home. In the evening, I might watch the TV or search the Net, whatever, just to pass the time. Occasionally, I will go to a ball game, college, or the pros, if a good game is scheduled. I also try to get to the gym at least once a week, to work out, but I haven't been going as often as I should lately."

I steeled myself and then asked, "What about girls? Are you seeing somebody?"

"There is no special girl. In fact, there never was a special girl. I dated a few girls but never seriously. I just could not find the right girl to get serious about. I met a girl once that I could have gotten serious with, but nothing came of it."

That is too bad, but good for me. He is not dating anyone now or even has an old girlfriend. Good. Though I enjoyed talking to him, I have to end this call, but on a pleasant note. "Martin, it has been genuinely nice chatting with you and getting to know a little about you. We must continue this conversation tomorrow. I still have a few errands to do tonight. Let us say goodnight now, and I'll see you tomorrow evening at 6:30."

"OK Mary. It was nice talking with you and getting to know a little about you also. I'll be at your place at 6:30, bye."

"Bye Martin."

I cradled the phone and danced around the room. He must like me and there is no one else in the way. It looks like this could develop into something special. Then a horrid thought came. He is going to come here. Here into this apartment and see this mess. I have to clean the whole place tonight. The apartment was usually clean and orderly, but I hadn't spent much time these last days on cleaning. My clothes were lying around as I had tried on different outfits. The mail and papers were strewn about. The kitchen was a mess, with dirty dishes and trash bags overrunning the counters. I preceded to rid up and organize.

Then I gave all the furniture a quick wax. What if he needs to use the bathroom? I removed all my undies and cosmetic aids. New towels were displayed, and the hamper emptied.

Should I have a snack ready when he comes in, or something ready when he brings me back? Should I offer him a drink, or a wine, when he enters? Oh, I never had these questions before, but I so want this to go right.

I decided on no snacks or drinks before we go out, but I will have some finger food ready and a bottle of wine in the fridge for when we return just in case he would want to stay for a while.

My plans were good. I will leave work early and stop off and pick up some food and a good wine. Then I will still have time to shower and dress in my most alluring new green outfit, that I was saving for something special like this. There will still be time for any last-minute items. Oh, I can't wait till tomorrow.

As I lay in bed thinking about tomorrow several more things to do, before he comes here, went through my mind. Should I have a bowl of fresh fruit displayed? Should there be a display of live flowers in the living room? Should I be ready when he calls or pretend to be a little bit tardy? I will have to ask the girls about these things, I thought as I drifted off to sleep.

CHAPTER 21

Martin

I have to break this phone silence somehow. Oh, why pretend. I'll just act as if we were alone somewhere, so I said, "It's like I've known you for a while and yet I don't know anything about you personally. I know I like talking with you, yet we are still practically strangers. If you aren't busy now, let's play a game?"

"A game? What kind of game?"

"Let me ask you a few questions, then if you want, you can ask me anything you want to. How does that sound?"

"Okay, but nothing too personal. Now me first. What's your full name?"

I replied, "Martin John Malone." That wasn't hard. Good, we were beginning to break the ice, although not really ice.

"Now it's still my turn. Where did you grow up?"

"I'm from a small town up the Allegany River, called Kittanning, it's an old Indian name. I left home to go to college, but I went back every weekend. I moved to the suburbs after college when I took this job that I have now." I didn't want to tell her that my family couldn't afford to send me to any schools out of the area or that I was still paying off my student loans and could only afford the small efficiency I live in now.

"What's your family like? Do you have any siblings?"

"My father works in a glass plant. My mother is a homemaker, but she does a lot of social work." No point in mentioning that my father is depressed and is hitting the bottle a lot lately. Or that my mother is working evening's part time, just to help out with the family finances. "I have a younger sister, Susie, she's a senior in high school and a brother, Jimmy, who's a sophomore at Penn State." I will not say that Jimmy is okay, but Susie is something else. She seems to want to be the most talked about girl in high school, with all her boyfriends, and the fast life she is leading, along with her poor grades. Mom is too busy with Dad to be able to control her. I think she is heading for a lot of trouble.

"Now it's my turn Mary. What's your full name?"

"It is Mary Agnes Burns. Don't you ever tell anyone my middle name. I am thinking of changing it. It is so old fashioned. Very few people know my middle name. I usually just use an initial."

"Mary Agnes. That is a real nice name. Not old fashion at all." It was a name fit for a sweet old-fashioned type of girl. Exactly right for a wholesome girl like Mary. "Where did you grow up?"

"I grew up in Charleston, WV. Went to all my schools there. I left to come to Pittsburgh to attend Chatham college. After graduation, the best job offers were from the Pittsburgh area, so I stayed in town and took an apartment near my old school."

"Tell me about your family."

"My father works in a chemical plant. My mother is a homemaker, but she was a schoolteacher. I have an older sister, Peggy. She is married but is having some problems with her husband right now. Then there is the twins, Kate and Kathy. They are just fifteen. All my sisters are living at home now."

That sounds like a nice family. Middle income, middle America. That is what produced such a nice girl like Mary. Should I ask some personal questions? Why not? If it is too personal, she does not have to answer. "What do you do in the evenings when you're not talking to me?"

"Nothing special. What every girl does. I fix myself something to eat. Do the dishes, clean house, and do the laundry once a week. All the usual mundane chores, then I go out with my friends a few times a week."

That sounds good so far. She is not dating someone seriously. Still going out with her friends, girlfriends, I hope. "Where do you go with your friends, when you go out?"

"Oh, nowhere in particular. Movies occasionally, and we frequent some of the single bars."

That sounds like she is not dating anyone now. Just going out with her girlfriends. This will be too personal, but I have to ask, "You're not dating anyone now, are you?"

"No, not now."

Yah, that is just great. No competition. The field is clear. I felt myself relax a little bit.

"It's my turn to ask the questions. What do you do after work?"

I hesitated before answering. Not wanting to lie but wanting to put my best foot forward. "After work, my three friends and myself usually go to some bar, to wait out the traffic jams. We pick a place where we can get something to eat along with our drinks after a few hours we split up and go home in the evening. I might watch TV or search the Net, whatever, just to pass the time. Occasionally I will go to a ball game, college, or the pros, if a good game is scheduled. I also try to go to the gym at least once a week to work out, but I haven't been going as often as I should lately." There all the truth but said to make me look better than I really am.

"What about girls? Are you seeing someone?"

"There's no special girl. In fact, there never was a special girl. I dated a few girls but never seriously. I just couldn't find the right one to get serious with. I met a girl once that I could have got serious with, but nothing came of it." I did not mention that stripper I met but who I wasn't ever able to find again. That how could I ever imagine getting serious with a stripper and whore. That entire episode has to be put aside and just considered drunken lust. It best be forgotten.

"Martin, it's been nice talking to you, and getting to know a little about you. I still have a few errands to do tonight. Let's say goodnight now, and I'll see you tomorrow at 6:30."

"Okay, Mary. It was nice talking with you and getting to know a little about you also. I will be at your place at 6:30. Bye."

"Bye, Martin."

What a great phone call. it was the best talk I ever had with a girl over the phone. Like we were old friends. We could ask personal questions and answer them without any embarrassment. Was it this way with a longtime girlfriend, or a wife? It was a new experience, talking to a girl like Mary. It felt comfortable. Like we belong together. Wow! What kind of thoughts were these? Am I getting serious about a girl that I hardly know? With that thought circulating through my mind, I plan my wardrobe for tomorrow, shine my best shoes, and dream myself to sleep. My dreams were all about Mary.

CHAPTER 22

I awoke to bright sunlight streaming through the bedroom window The rays were glittering off the glass bottles and crystals on the dresser. The whole room was sparkling. Oh, what a glorious day it is, and it is just going to get better by tonight.

After my shower and morning absolutions, I dressed in an ordinary business suit. I would change after work into that new green dress for tonight. I had my usual breakfast of orange juice, bagel with cream cheese and a cup of decafe. As I passed the hall mirror, I paused to take stock of myself. Here I stood, twenty-three years old, college educated and still a virgin. Oh, there had been instances where in a deep passionate embrace, I almost said yes, but I can barely remember the boy's name now.

Looking at myself, I saw a woman, five feet and 5 inches tall, with very good posture, as my mother still keeps telling me. My weight is 123 1bs. which is good for my height. I have a good figure, well proportioned, 35-26-35 which is not too bad. My cup size is just a B, but my bras have been getting tighter lately. I might have to start wearing a C cup. My gosh, if they keep growing like this, what will I look like at age forty? A size DD cup?

My appraisal continued. Hair medium brown, slight wave, worn below the ears. Eyes green, but never needing glasses. Teeth all there with just a few cavities, all corrected. The teeth were straight and white and I have been told many times that I had a beautiful smile. My eyes were my best feature, especially when wearing eye makeup.

Overall, the mirror told me that this was a terrific woman here, just waiting for the right man. Hopefully after tonight, I will know if Martin is that man.

The morning at work went fast, in kind of a happy glow. Sometimes I was giddy and other times I started to worry about tonight. Most of the time I was just in a happy dream.

Lunch with Janet and Dolly was filled with laughter and with their crude jokes about what Martin and I would be doing tonight. When we returned to work, they wished me luck and went to their offices. I decided to take the rest of the day off by using some vacation time.

Walking past the new department store, I entered and went to their famous beauty salon. I told the receptionist I wanted a bright new hair style but not too different. I told her I had a very important date tonight.

When they finished and I looked into a mirror, I was startled at my fresh look. My hair was now shorter, cut around the ears with lots of curls, and it was several shades lighter. It looked good, just what I wanted. I had never wom this style before. I looked like one of those old-time movie stars, cannot remember her name now. All the girls at the salon assured me that I looked great, and my date would find me different but extremely attractive.

On the way home I purchased a bottle of wine and some stuff to make snacks for tonight.

I again cleaned the apartment, made the snacks, and put the wine in the fridge to cool.

Everything was ready but me. I showered, being careful of my new hair style, shaved my legs and under my arms. I put on my newest and laciest bra and panties and a new pair of pantyhose. I applied my sexiest and most expensive perfume to my neck, along my arms and between my breasts. I also put a dab on my belly- button for good luck.

It was approaching six o'clock as I was finishing my makeup. I donned my new green dress with the low back and a semi plunging neckline. The green was supposed to match the color of my eyes but it looked different now. I put on a pair of small gold earrings which surprisingly looked particularly good with my new shorter hair. A gold necklace completed the look. With the matching short green jacket, I looked as good as I possible could. I then put on my new pair of green pumps. Hopefully, they would be broken in enough. What I do not need tonight is a pair of shoes that hurt. I checked myself in the mirror and approved of my fresh look. He better like what he sees when he looks at me, after all this trouble and planning.

I removed the jacket and placed it across the sofa, sat down and waited. I immediately jumped up and turned on the stereo and played some soft mood music. I don't even know what kind of music he likes. I smiled to myself as I remembered he liked Arabic music. I again sat down and composed myself. At six twenty-five the buzzer rang.

Jumping up, I went to open the door, when the buzzer rang again, and I realized it was the front door to the building. I pressed the button to open the front door and sat down again. Not nervous am I. Ha! That is the first time I mistook the buzzer for the door since I have lived here.

There was a knock on the door and when I opened it, Martin stood there. As tall and as good-looking as I remembered and carrying flowers. Roses! Red roses.

"Hello Martin. Come in."

CHAPTER 23

Martin

When I awoke my head was splitting. I had tossed and turned all night. I dreamed about Mary all night but it was a series of nightmares. Not really nightmares but of things going wrong and me making all kinds of stupid mistakes. Totally spoiling the entire evening. What a night.

The day continued being bad. First, I cut my neck while shaving and the blood just flowed for minutes. I have a bright red scar on my neck now. I forgot to do the laundry and I was down to my last pair of clean underwear. Should I save them for tonight and wear a used pair to work?

No, I will wear the clean pair to work, and I will have to shop at lunch time for a few more pairs.

When making breakfast, just juice and cereal, the milk was sour, and the juice was starting to smell. That did not help my stomach as I was having loose bowels all morning. If I didn't calm down I will ruin the whole night. It will be just like those bad dreams I had. I toasted some stale bread and drank some black coffee and that settled me down.

Taking my car to work I narrowly avoided two accidents that I almost caused. Just lack of concentration. I put thoughts of Mary and tonight out of mind and safely followed the traffic on the parkways to my parking spot near my building. Trying to concentrate on my work was difficult but I muddled through it without making too many errors. I will have to double check it Monday.

At lunch with Bubba, Ron and Chuck, my nerves started to relax. Maybe it was their good natured kidding or it could have been the large bowl of soup I had, the first food of the day.

When the soup settled my stomach and wanted to stay there, I then ordered a small steak and salad.

Walking back to work I felt good. I noticed the sun was shining which made my plans for the evening work out better. Suddenly I relaxed and for the first time really believed tonight would be a wonderful night with a wonderful girl.

After work I rushed out to beat the traffic and arrived home early. Things were getting better. As I was parking the car, I remembered the underwear. Quickly backing out I raced to the nearby mall and entered the closest store. There I purchased several packages of shorts and undershirts and also a few pairs of socks. The mall was not crowded at this time and the whole trip took only a few minutes. Arriving home, I realized I was just a few minutes later than my normal arrival time, but still running a little late.

I showered and shaved again. This time being careful and not cutting myself. I applied hair tonic, the type with no odor and brushed my hair carefully. I applied deodorant and just a splash of my best after shave lotion. Then I donned my new underwear and socks. I wore a long-sleeved white shirt with cuff links, gray trousers, and a navy-blue sport coat. The whole effect looked too somber, so I decided on a bright red and blue tie.

It was almost six when I left my apartment just in time to buy half dozen red roses from the vendor along the highway and speed to the Oakland section of Pittsburgh. It looks like I will be on time as all the traffic is going the opposite direction. I found Mary's building, easily parked, and walked to the front entrance. She was listed as M Burns. I rang the buzzer and the door unlatched. I entered and took the elevator to the third floor and found her door, 324. Taking a deep breath, I knocked. When the door opened and I saw Mary, all beautiful and smiling, with a head full of curls. The lights from the couch at her back shown dimly. She looked like an Angel with a Halo.

"Hello Martin. Come on in."

CHAPTER 24

Handing her the roses, I said, "Hello Mary. These are for you."

"Well thank you, Martin. They are lovely." I reached for them and brought them to me and inhaled. "They smell wonderful. I'll put them in a vase now." As I fussed with the flowers and the quick arrangement in the vase, I wondered, should I have greeted him with a little quick kiss on the cheek? "I'll set them here on the kitchen table where I can see them from all parts of the apartment."

Martin was still standing near the door looking awkwardly and not at ease. I went toward him, reached out for his hand, and brought him into the center of the living room. "I'm forgetting my manners. Come in and sit down."

Watching her as she moved about the room, so beautiful. so comfortable in these rooms. A strange feeling went through me. This is where she belongs. Not necessarily here, but in a home with a family round her and me around her. "This is a lovely place you have here. It is decorated very nice. But you look different. You changed your hair."

It took him a long enough to notice. "Yes, I changed the style a little bit. It was something I was planning to do for a while." I lied. "How do you like it?" I shook my head and slowly turn around.

She looked older, more mature. Not like the free-spirited girl I bumped into at lunch. She might be in a lot of trouble if she gets out in the rain now. "It looks great. In fact, everything about you looks great. When you spun around like that, you looked like you could be a dancer in some Hollywood movie." The whole effect, shoes. low cut dress, hairstyle, everything was glamorous. In fact, she was intoxicating. I've could have sat there and just stared at her.

A dancer in a movie! Is he starting to remember? But I look so different now, from that time when I stripped. He cannot remember me now. "Thank you. I am ready now. All I need is my jacket." I reached down and picked up the jacket and started to put it on.

"Let me help you with that."

I rushed over to her, and taking the jacket from her delicate hands, held it while she placed her arms through the sleeves. The aroma of her perfume was quite exciting. Sweet, yet sensual. As she stretched backward slightly, to place her arms in the sleeves, I noticed the swell of her breasts in that low cut dress. They were larger than I had imagined and very sexy. I had this impulse to place my hand over them. I took a deep breath and stepped back.

"Thank you." I let him place the jacket on me and the places where his hands touched my bare skin was intoxicating. I am glad I wore this dress with so much of me showing. The smell of him was still around me as we walked out the door. Taking the elevator to the lobby, he held my hand. Not too tight, but not like a friend either. He walked me to his car, a black coupe very shiny and clean, and held the door open for me. It was a neat acrobatic feat to enter and slide into the seat without my dress rising high on my thigh. Unfortunately, I am not a neat acrobat, and my dress did ride up high on my thigh. I glanced up at Martin and his eyes were diverted. Very much like a gentleman. That made me feel good. He was a perfect gentleman. He closed the door and while he walked around to his side, I had a different thought. I wish he had seen my legs. They are quite shapely and tonight they have my best hose to show them off.

As she closed the apartment door and we walked to the elevator, I did not know what to do. Hold her hand or put my arm around her. I hesitated, then did nothing, till we were at the elevator door. I gently put my arm around her while I pressed the call button for the lobby. The door opened immediately and when we entered, I took her hand in mine. She made no move to remove it. We had a short but very sweet ride down. I continue to hold her hand as we walked to my car. It looked new and shiny under the streetlight. I am glad I cleaned and washed it last night. I opened the passenger door and held it while Mary slid into the seat. Her dress slid up and I saw a lot of leg and just a glimpse of lace undergarments. I quickly adverted my eyes to not embarrass her, if she would happen to glance up at me, then closed the door.

While walking around the car to my side, I could not get that erotic intoxicating sight out of my mind. Embarrassment set in, as I noticed that I had an erection, so I fumbled with the car door for a few extra seconds, till I calmed down, then slid in beside her.

"Your car looks nice. Is it new?"

"It's almost three years old but I don't drive it much. Just a couple of miles a day and park it indoors at work and at home, so it does not get very dirty." I am glad I took the time to spruce it up last night. We drove down the East Parkway, along the Monongahela River till we got to the Point. I took the Fort Pitt Bridge South but turned before the huge tunnel and started to follow the Ohio River.

"I thought we would go to the top of Mount Washington a different way."

"Any way is fine, Martin. I still get a little confused when I get away from downtown, I guess it is from not having my own car and not getting around by myself."

We turned into this dark unpaved lot and drove till we came to this huge structure. There were people milling about. To calm any fears Mary might have about this place, I started to explain where we were. "If you have never been here, this is the Duquesne Incline."

"No, I've never been here. I heard about it and often seen those little cars climbing the mountain. They remind me of the cable cars in San Francisco, but these cars are always level."

We entered the depot and I purchased two roundtrip tickets. Taking Mary's hand, I led her into the waiting car. We took a seat and waited while the car remained inside the depot. We had no view. When the car started with a jolt, Mary let out a gasp and took my hand, squeezing it tightly. The car started to move very slowly and gently.

"This is so exciting. This car is so much bigger than when seen from the city below. Oh look. We can see the Point and all the buildings downtown. There's River Stadium and it is all lit up. Are the Pirates playing tonight?"

Still holding her hand, I said. "Yes, they are home tonight. Are you enjoying this?"

"Yes. I'm glad we came this way."

The car slowed, bounced, and jerked then finally stopped in the upper depot and we departed. We strolled around to the observation deck and stopped to read the memorabilia.

"We still have a few minutes till our reservation time and the restaurant is close. Would you like to look out onto the scene for a few minutes?"

"Yes. I'd like that."

We went to the railing and scanned the beautiful view. I noticed Mary gave a slight shiver, so I placed my arm around her shoulders. She did not say anything but just cuddled a little closer.

"Look, you can see where I work, and the fountain, and all the ferryboats. The city looks beautiful when it is all lit up."

Yes, it is beautiful. I was looking at Mary, not the view beyond. After a few minutes, I said, "We better get moving."

Taking her hand in mine, we left the observation deck and strolled the short distance to the restaurant. Like two lovers on a romantic holiday.

This is such a romantic start to the evening. Martin has such good taste in showing a girl around the town. I hope it is not from a lot of practice with other girls. We entered the restaurant and were seated at a window table overlooking the whole beautiful scene. "This is nice Martin. I really like this place. It's so pretty here and tonight, so clear you can see for miles."

It is pretty here. What makes it pretty is looking at Mary, with the city in the background. "Yes, it is pretty here. This view from Mount Washington is the best place to see Pittsburgh."

"Would you like a drink before dinner?"

"Yes. I would like a glass of wine. I do not usually have a drink with every meal but dining with you is going to turn me into an alcoholic." I smiled at his obvious discomfort, then added, "I'm going to have to cut one of them out."

"Please, please, cut out the drinking not dining with me."

He looked so disheartened, that I reached out and took his hand, and said, "I was only joking."

We had a leisurely appetizer of white wine followed by shrimp cocktail. We both then ordered the same entrée, filet mignon with creamed asparagus as a side dish. We even like the meat prepared the same way, medium rare. I commented during the excellent meal we have a lot of similarities in our food and its reputation. "We seem to like the same things, Mary. Hope we never disagree about anything."

I smiled as he said that as I was eating my steak, I really prefer my meat well done. I ordered it his way just to make a good impression. We are never going to have any kind of a future together if he thinks a couple must always like the same things.

"I hope we never disagree about anything important, Martin, but don't you think a minor difference is good?"

"Thinking about it your way makes sense. We are two completely different people, yet we seem to blend together."

Blend together! What does he mean by that? Is he implying some kind of intimate sexual blend? The way I feel right now, all he has to do is ask and I'll fling myself into his arms. Needing to repress this urge, I added, "I think minor difference make a relationship more interesting. Even when a minor disagreement occurs, there's always the fun part of making up." I smiled at that bit of my mother's wisdom.

"Well, let us agree not to disagree tonight. Let's keep tonight special."

While the waiter cleared our table, we ordered dessert. It was our first difference. Mary ordered a chocolate cheesecake while I ordered a slice of peach pie. We both ordered cappuccino.

When the waiter left, Mary laughed at me and said, "I hope this will not spoil your life, but we do have our differences. If it will make you feel better, you can have a taste of my cake. But I want a taste of your pie in return."

Her smile and laughter made me feel good, being teased by Mary. It seemed to make our relationship a little bit stronger, as if we had known each other for a lot longer than just these few days.

While we shared our desserts amid burst of laughter, I began to relax. Maybe it was the two glasses of wine, or it could have been Martin's attitude. At the beginning, he seemed a bit reserved. Nice and gentle but holding back something. He is different now. Much more relaxed and natural. It is like his real personality is appearing. I like him much more now if that is possible.

As dinner neared the end, I glance at the time. It was after 9:30. I paid the bill and we walked back to the incline depot, arms around each other, in a kind of semi embrace. Looking over the panoramic view I noticed the ball game was over. People were walking near the stadium and throughout the downtown as well. I had wanted a quiet spot to be alone with Mary.

"It looks like the game is over. All the places in Station Square will be quite crowded. They will be filled with noisy drunken people now. Would you like to go someplace else?"

"I don't feel like crowds now. Why don't you just take me home. We can relax there, and I have a bottle of wine chilling, and there are some snacks also. Besides, I ate too much cheesecake to go dancing now." Taking the initiative, I pushed him towards the cable car, but being careful not to remove my arm from around his sexy body.

We entered the car, and my every intention was to kiss her then and there, but the car was filling with the after-dinner crowd, so we just rode down, admiring the view, with our arms around each other.

CHAPTER 25

Debarking, we stroll toward my car, still hand in hand. I wanted to stop and kiss her here, but in the darkness and among the other people, I decided to wait. As I held the door open for Mary, I again got a glance of her long legs and a brief view of lace. This time the sight was longer as Mary took a lot more time getting into the seat. I did not avert my eyes this time, as I was not feeling so gentlemanly.

Returning to my side, I felt a twinge of remorse for selecting this car model. This car is not the place to kiss a girl for the first time. The bucket seats with the high center console make romantic kissing difficult. I will wait till we get to her place.

Sliding into the car seat, I deliberately took my time. As my dress rode up my leg, I let it ride up higher than before, and took my time adjusting the skirt but did not look up to see if Martin is looking. I hope he is and gets a good look. After all, my legs are some of my better features. During the ride to my place, I had a startling thought. I purposely did that. Showed Martin my legs. I never have done that before at least, not intentionally. What am I becoming? Am I just getting desperate for a man, any man, and will do anything, even strip to try to get a man to like me? Or is it Martin, causing me to do these things?

Trying desperately to get him to like me. These wonton actions are so uncharacteristic of me. What will I do when we get to my apartment? The various thoughts going through my mind made me feel weak, so I indulged myself and reached over and placed my hand on Martin's arm and gently squeezed.

"I had a wonderful time tonight, Martin. Thank you."

The way back to her apartment took longer than expected. We had to pass through the city and it is normal, that after any event, gridlock occurs, along with pedestrians blocking most intersections. The trip was pleasant since at every stop we held hands. Every time I reached for Mary's hand, it was there, and she always gave my hand a sweet squeeze. Once through the downtown area, we held hands while I drove one handed till we reached her building. I quickly parked and hurried to go around the car to open the door.

It was such a sweet ride back home, we held hands all the way. I tried to show him how I felt in a little way by gently squeezing his hand at every opportunity. I hope that was starting to turn him on a bit. We hardly spoke during a short trip, but it was an intimate feeling, alone in a car and holding hands. Vastly different from the trip earlier this evening.

What will happen once we got inside my place? I definitely will not let him leave without kissing me. Kissing me a lot and letting him do other things to me too. The way I feel, he can do anything he wants, and I just might help. I might do some things to him. This could be the night I lose my virginity. It would be about time, and I am glad I waited so Martin would be the first. First? Do I think there will be more men in my life after Martin? I cannot imagine something like that happening.

Martin stopped the car in front of the entrance and hurried to open the door. How courteous. Just to inflame him a little bit more, and to give myself a naughty feeling, I will give him a good show when I get out. My gosh. Here I go again, being naughty. What kind of a girl am I becoming?

Opening and holding the door, I held out my hand to assist Mary. She held my hand and swung her legs around and slid out of the seat. Her skirt rode all the way up her legs and a lot of legs showed. She did not move for a second but just looked at me, then left the car in one final swing and clung to my arm. The sight of her almost bare thighs caused an immediate reaction, which I tried to hide, by walking slightly behind her, all the way to the elevator.

Purposely sliding and swinging my legs in one motion, I felt my skirt ride high on the thighs. I hesitated, looked at Martin and saw him staring at my legs. I decided to stop in this position for a second, to let him have a good look, before exiting the car. He closed the door, but I clung to his arm all the way to the elevator. I brushed my breast against his arm at every chance I had. I felt deliciously naughty. The way I had felt at the beginning of my private strip dance for Martin.

Desire for Mary was starting to overwhelm me. I wanted to grab hold of her and passionately kiss her now, here in the lobby. As I reached for her, my opportunity slipped away, as an elderly couple entered the lobby and approached the elevator. The ride to the third floor was silent and made with proper decorum.

Waiting for the elevator, with our hands clasped, I raised my face to Martin and leaned toward him, expecting a kiss. Our first kiss. Then damn it, the couple from the fourth floor entered the lobby and stood beside us. We backed away and rode the elevator in silence.

Walking to my door but still holding hands, I managed to extract the key and handed it to Martin. He fumbled, trying to open the door, as I still had his other hand and teasingly would not let go.

We walked quickly to her door, still holding hands. At her door, she handed me her key but would not let go of my other hand. It took a few moments to open the door as she playfully pulled and tugged at my hand, while I tried to turn the key and the doorknob at the same time, using only one hand. Finally, I managed to open the door and Mary squeezed past me, very slowly. Saying, "Let me get the lights." Both her breasts rub against my chest as she entered the room. I made no attempt to back away.

I'll turn on only the table lamps. It will be dimmer, more romantic. Turning, I saw Martin, still standing by the door, looking handsomely as ever. Walking slowly toward him, I stopped inches away placed my hands on his arms, I raised my face, looked into his eyes, and then slowly mouthed these words. Kiss Me.

Watching Mary walk around the room, I was mesmerized by her grace and charm. I wanted to rush to her, clutch her in my arms, and passionately kiss her. Instead, I just stood here, looking awkward and uncertain. Mary turned, looked at me and slowly walked to me, stopping inches away. She then placed her hands on my arms, looked up to me, and slowly and soundlessly, said, "Kiss Me."

Putting my hands on her shoulders I leaned down and gently place my lips upon hers. Something strange, yet pleasant occurred. The heat from our lips was like an intense fire, sensual, erotic, intoxicating and all-consuming. My hands pulled her body to me as I crushed my lips to hers. Her lips responded with their own pressure while her entire body merged into mine. Her breasts were flattened against me, and I could feel the swell of her belly pressed against me. I had an immediate erection which was pressing against her. We continued to kiss without a second of relaxing, while the feeling from the kiss became more intense.

Martin placed his hands on my arms and leaning forward placed his lips upon mine while he pulled me toward him. His lips upon mine created such a warm dizzying feeling. The strange heat that passed between us was intense and momentarily I felt faint. I pressed my lips hard against his lips and tried to mold my body to his. My breasts were crushed against his chest and our lower bodies were completely together. Standing on tiptoe, I pressed my body harder against him. I could feel his manhood rising and throbbing. That excited me more. I slowly opened my lips. Using my tongue, I explored his lips over and over. Then moving my tongue faster and faster, I darted into and out of his slowly opening lips. The feeling was delicious and very sensual.

The kiss lasted longer and longer, becoming more intense with each passing second. Time seemed to stop. My senses were reeling as our bodies, so tightly meshed started to sway. Suddenly, a thought entered my mind. I am breathing. I have never kissed a girl this long, continuously, without our lips parting. Yet, with Mary's sweet lips against mine, I didn't have to break away to breathe.

I felt Mary's lips slowly parting and her tongue starting to caress my lips. The feeling of excitement and sexual arousal became intense. A feeling of lust, pure wanton desire, began to build inside of me. Only my feelings for her kept me from throwing her down on the floor and having my way with her. Repressing these urges, I instead, slowly opened my lips to her darting tongue. Such sensual feelings that pulsated through my body were new to me. I have French kissed girls before and had them reciprocate, but never with this much pleasure or sensual arousal. My tongue began to explore her sweet mouth while my hands moved over her bare back, pressing her harder to me. One hand was under her jacket while the other was rubbing and squeezing the swell of her ass.

The kiss lasted and lasted. Martin's tongue and mine were playing games inside each other's mouths. I felt like never stopping. My arms were around his neck pulling my body up and into his. When his hand slipped under my jacket and started the explorer my bareback, the feeling that it caused was like fire on my skin. I gave a silent thanks that I had decided to wear this low-cut dress. Then when his other hand roamed down to my lower back, and then even lower, the feelings of arousal that came over me were intense and animal like. Then he started to rub and squeeze and massage my buttocks. I almost fainted with desire. This caused me to emit small moans and to slowly move my lower body in a circular motion against Martin, while pressing harder and harder against him.

Time seemed to stand still. Minutes pasted. I was getting very flushed, and a wetness was forming in my vagina. A strange yet pleasant feeling. Sensual and wanton. All my defenses and inhibitions were gone. I wanted to drop backward to the floor and letting Martin have his way with me. Yet, some small thought was going through my mind, distracting my pleasure.

Is this the way I want to lose my virginity? On the floor, by the front door, with my clothes on? No, not this way. I gently removed my arms from Martin's neck, backed an inch away and separated our lips. I experienced such a feeling of loss, that I immediately started kissing him again, then stopped. His hands were still upon me, but their sexual movement stopped. We just held each other and let our breathing get back to normal.

"That was great, Martin. I am going to want more of the same, a lot more. Let's take a break for a minute."

The feelings this gave me were intense and very sensual, but there was something else, a feeling of warmth along with the fiery passion. A feeling I had never felt before. Lust, animal desire, and yet a feeling of tenderness, of not wanting to harm her. A quick thought flashed through my mind. I did not bring any protection with me. I never have asked the girl to supply them, as that was always seemed not the right thing to do. Damn it. I never thought this relationship would progress this far tonight. I will worry about that later as I was still getting extreme pleasure from this kiss. My roving hands were probing further, and Mary's body was throbbing against me with a passion that was undeniable. Her body signs indicated she wanted me as much as I wanted her. I was getting ready to lower her body to the floor when she gently removed her arms from around my neck and backed a fraction of an inch away. She then withdrew her tongue and stopped the kiss. The feeling of sadness I felt quickly went away as Mary started to kiss me again. Then she stopped and lowered her head against my heaving chest.

We just held each other for a while, then she said, "That was great, Martin. I am going to want more of the same, a lot more. Let's take a break for a minute." She relaxed slightly but still was pressed to me. I didn't want this embrace to stop.

Good. We feel the same. "Okay Mary, let's take a break, but not for too long."

We separated and I took his hand and led him to the sofa. "Sit down here and get comfortable."

When I sat down, she jumped onto my lap and kissed me passionately for a few seconds, then pushed my arms away and arose with a little laugh, and said, "More later. I just wanted to see if it was a good sitting down as it was standing up. It was."

CHAPTER 26

66 Just sit there and don't go away. I have to take a few
minutes to catch my breath. I'll be right back." With a
smile and a childish shaking of my finger at him, I hurried
to the bathroom. I needed time to analyze my feelings. All my
emotions were in a whirl. I was slightly dizzy from his kisses,
and I had this strange yet wonderful wetness between my legs.
Looking at myself in the mirror, I saw that I was a wreck. My
newly coiffed hair was messy and the new curls all array. What
lipstick I had left was smeared. I had to repair myself.

I decided to brush my hair and fix my curls. I removed my
earrings and brushed my teeth. Removing my jacket, I applied
some deodorant and added just a trace of perfume. The jacket
was just getting in the way, so I decided to leave it off.

My breathing and heartbeat were back to normal. As I sat on
the edge of the bath, I pondered my next moves. After all, this
could affect my whole future. Should I return to Martin and
throw myself on him? Again, playing this wanted woman and
letting him make love to me? I know he wants to make love to
me. I could tell from all his body motions. Every part of my
body wants him. Wants him so bad. I can hardly stay here and
only think about it.

Then everything Dolly and Janet told me about having sex on the first date went through my mind. Even if you are sure, you have the right man in your arms at the time, somehow things change the next morning. Ecstasy of love is replaced by guilt and a change in the man's attitude toward you occur. You feel cheap and are treated with a little or no respect. The chances of future dates are slim or none. The man calls not for a date but only for explicit sex.

Deep down inside me, I feel that this is different. This is for real. This is true love. Martin's feeling for me seemed genuine and he has been such a gentleman tonight. I am sure he won't change tomorrow. Should I take the chance and make Love to Martin, or should I repress all these bursting emotions and hold him at arm's length? Well, not that far away.

Deciding to avert any sex tonight, if it is at all possible, I hurried from the bath, dropped my jacket and earrings off in my bedroom, and returned to my Martin.

"Martin, as much as I like you kisses, let's take a break for a few minutes. Okay?"

He rose from the sofa looking dejected, spread his hands, and said, "All right Mary, anything you say. But did I do something wrong?"

He was so sad looking, that I approached him and kissed him full on the lips. Then quickly backed away. His looks changed to happy yet confused. "We were going a little too fast. My emotions were getting in the way of my better judgment. Let's slow down a little bit." Taking his hand, I led him back to the sofa and said, "Sit here while I fix it as a snack and some drinks."

Not waiting for an answer, I went to the kitchen and opened the bottle of wine and got two of my best wine glasses. Took the cheese and fruit from the fridge and adding crackers to the tray, I carried it out to Martin. It was a good plan, having all this arranged. It will cool the flames without being too cool to him. Carrying the tray, I suddenly thought, this is my first meal I am serving him, but it is not going to be my last.

Setting the tray down, I went around the table and sat next to him on the sofa. Very close. So, close our hips were touching. That should let him know I still have feelings for him. "I hope you like the snacks? Would you pour the wine, Martin, please?"

CHAPTER 27

Martin

After Mary left the room, I sat there wondering what went wrong? Everything was just like in my dreams, only better. I didn't make the first move; she beat me to it. She started the tongue kissing first. My hands were not violating any part of her, no matter how much I wanted to do things to her body. What was wrong? She could not be shy. Not the way she kisses. They were the most sensual and erotic kisses that I have ever had. She must have had a lot of experience kissing men. After all, she is a beautiful and desirable woman, and many men must have kissed her before. That thought gave me a quick moment of resentment, but it quickly passed.

Was she just leading me on? No. She was not that kind of a girl. Was she a tease? I have met several like that before, but Mary is different.

At least, these moments apart were letting me cool down. My reaction has subsided, and I can think rationally again. I will just sit here and wait for her return and see what happens next. She did not seem mad or insulted, so maybe she just had to relieve herself. She did not look angry, and she said to not go away, so it could be that nothing is wrong.

Sitting there frustrated, I decided to loosen my tie. It was twisted all around my collar anyway. Standing up, I removed my jacket also. I folded it and laid it on the arm of the sofa, then I decided to place it across the chair instead in case the sofa would be romantically used later.

The minutes Mary was away dragged on. It seemed like hours had passed but I knew it had it only been a few minutes. My thoughts returned to that passionate embrace by the door. That first kiss was the most passionate, the most sensual, the most erotic, the most emotionally draining kiss I ever had. It was also the longest kiss I had ever experienced. For all that time our lips never parted. Never had I kissed a girl for any length of time without our lips parting while we took a breath. How did I breathe during the kiss? It lasted for several minutes, so I know I must have taken a breath somehow. It was all just a sweet yet erotic remembrance. One that will never be forgotten.

Turning, I saw Mary exit the bathroom and go to the bedroom carrying her jacket. Returning to me, she looked refreshed and still incredibly beautiful and quite sexy. She stood over me, smiled and said, "Martin, as much as I like your kisses, let's take a break for a few minutes. Okay?"

Good, she is not mad, and I think she means to resume the kissing part soon. Rising I spread out my hands for her and said, "All right Mary. Anything you say. But did I do something wrong?"

She looked concerned at those words, then gave a slight grin, approached very close to me, and kissed me full on the lips. Then she broke off and backed away. Still smiling, she said, "I think we were going a little too fast. My emotions were getting in the way of my better judgment. Let's slow down a little." She gently took my hands and led me back to the sofa, saying, "Sit here while I fix us a snack and some drinks."

Not waiting for my reply, she turned and went into the kitchen and started making very pleasant domestic noises. Sitting there, my mind and emotions were still whirling in confusion. First it was the sweet kiss and warm embrace, a feeling of romance and bliss. Then that most erotic kiss, a feeling of raw passion. When she broke away, a feeling of frustration and loss. That quick kiss on the sofa, the feeling of romance and desire again. When she left the room a feeling of loss, worry and frustration. Then when she returned and kissed me quickly, again a feeling of romance, desire, and lust. Now she is preparing food for me, a feeling of romance and something else. Like contentment, romance, lust, and desire, all rolled together. Could this be how love feels?

My thoughts were broken as Mary returned, carrying a tray with glasses and a wine bottle. She placed the tray down the and sat on the sofa and squeeze' remarkably close to me. Our hips and thighs were touching. She said sweetly, "Would you pour the wine, Martin?"

CHAPTER 28

He looked so right sitting there. His hair slightly mussed, tie off, in my apartment, on my sofa and next to me. Was it my dreams coming true or just wishful thinking, plus a little desire? There was a lot of desire, deep down inside me. Something I had never felt before, but it feels so right and good. I just felt like the purring, I was so contented.

Her warm body was so near and soft against my leg that I almost spilled the wine. Taking the two glasses, I handed one to her, and not being able to think of anything else to say, just said, "To us." She smiled, took a small sip, then leaned toward me, raised her face and I kissed her as softly and as gently as I could. This kiss was all tenderness and romance and lasted only a few seconds, but it caused a new strange, wonderful feeling in me. A feeling of tenderness, kindness and yes, passion too. Another feeling was there also. I wanted to hold and protect her, to keep her from harm to take care of her. Was this love?

That kiss was sweet, yet it started to kindle those feelings of passion deep inside of me. I raise my glass and say, "Martin, it's my turn to propose a toast. May this feeling we have tonight never end." That was a bold statement, but it is how I felt. We raised our glasses, and each took only a sip, then he leaned over and kissed me gently. This kiss lasted longer and longer, our lips parted, and our tongues started playing games again. I felt Martin putting his glass down and as his arms went around me, I somehow was caught with my glass pressed against my breast and couldn't move in his embrace. I finally pulled my lips away and whispered, "Martin, my glass."

Quickly releasing her, I took her glass and placed it on the table and turned to resume the embrace. I noticed a widening stain on her dress right between her heaving breasts. "Oh, I'm so sorry. I spilled your wine. Let me wipe it up." I started to reach for my handkerchief, but Mary's hand stopped me.

"No. Don't wipe it off. It will be best if I sponge it off. Just sit here while I take care of it. I will be back in a minute. Don't go away." I hurried to the bath and examined the dress. It is the prettiest and most expensive dress I ever owned, now possibly ruined. But it served its purpose. I got my man, at least I think I have Martin.

The wine stain was large and covered most of the front of my dress. I could not let Martin see me like this. I will have to change but to what? Jeans? A blouse? No, too casual. Pajamas? No too intimate. I do not want him to think I am ready to hop into bed with him, and on the first real date. Even if I am ready, but we will just have to wait. I know, I will wear that new set of fancy lounging pajamas. They look more like a party outfit, than pajamas. Besides, they are so bright and colorful, they look like a lounging outfit. Why am I always either getting undressed for him, or intentionally showing my body to this man? It is a new feeling I have when I am near him.

As I removed my ruined dress, I consider removing my bra also, to let Martin feel my bare breasts against him. Reluctantly, I decided against that. Dressed in the pajamas, I surveyed myself in a mirror. The pajamas looked good. Not like pajamas at all. I applied a little cologne and returned to my Martin.

What a klutz I am. To spill wine onto her dress. It must have cost a lot. Should I offer to have it cleaned or to replace it. No, that just does not seem the right thing to do tonight. Maybe I'll make the offer at a later date. What is taking her so long? Is she going to be mad at me? No, she did not appear to mad at me, just worried about her dress.

Here she comes and she changed to another outfit. It looks like she is wearing pajamas. They are so bright and full figured. They probably are some kind of party dress. "You look great, Mary. I hope your dress isn't ruined."

"No, I think the wine will come out, but I had to change out of that wet outfit. Do you like it?" I said as I spun around for him.

"Yes. It looks great."

"It is pajamas, but it also is a hostess dress." Now why did I have to say pajamas? "Why don't you refresh my wine glass?" I smiled as sweetly as I could and sat down beside him, our hips touching. Looking up at his eyes, I said softly, "Where were we?"

I placed her glass on the table carefully, and slowly encircle her in my arms, and kiss her gently on the lips. Every time she started to open her sweet lips, I would back off, by removing my lips for a second. Then I slowly began to kiss her again. Finally, she wrapped her arms around my neck and forcefully thrust her lips to mine, with a probing incessant tongue, demanding all of my mouth.

Minutes passed, as our bodies molded intimately from head to foot. Reluctantly, I withdrew from Martins embrace and place my cheek against his. I whispered into his ear, "Don't tease me like that. Martin, I can't stand being teased by you, as if you didn't want to kiss me. Don't you like kissing me?"

"Of course, I like kissing you. Can't you tell?"

Of course, I could tell, and he was also aroused, as I easily felt his erection throbbing against my thigh. With the most extreme effort, I slowly untangle myself and sit upright and say, "We have to slow down a little. We are going too fast. Let us just have a drink so I can cool down. I reached for his glass and slowly held it to his lips, while he took a small sip, then I leaned forward and gently kissed his lips. "Did you like that drink?" I teased.

"I liked it very much. Why don't you try one?" I said, as I raised her glass to her sweet lips and held it there while she took a drink. Then I wiped her lips with my tongue, and gently kissed her eager lips.

"That was delicious. I'll have another, the same way."

We continue this ritual into the night. Bodies near, extremely near but not touching. Lips just kissing but only after a sip or small bite of food. The evening became very intimate. While my body was aching with desire for him, I was becoming slightly tipsy and thoroughly in love with him. If he would have reached for me, fondled my breast, or placed his hand between my thighs, I would not have resisted. I would have helped and encouraged him. First date be damned. I wanted him. When I would lean toward him, I tried to brush my breast against his arm or chest. Oh, I should have removed my bra when I had the chance.

When the bottle was empty, I stood to get another, but I swayed and nearly fell. I sat down on Martin's lap, kissed him heartly and said, "Would you get the other bottle out of the refrigerator, please?"

I gently remove my arms from around her body, and my hands from her breasts, where they accidentally found themselves, when I caught her. Kissing her while I slowly untangled myself, I gently placed her on a sofa. She languidly stretched and lay back seductively. She whispered into my ear, "Don't take too long."

Finding the bottle was not much trouble, but I had to hunt for the corkscrew. I finally found it in the sink. Opening the bottle, I hurried back to Mary.

"I like a taste of that one, with the same ending." she said with a grin.

I stood staring down at her, so beautiful, so sweet, so soft and yet so sexy, and so wanton in her seductive position. Laying on the sofa, arms outstretched, beckoning for me. I wanted her more than I have ever dreamt that I could want a woman. She gave no impression that she would refuse any of my sexual advances or deny my desires. In fact, gave me the impression she would welcome them. Yet I held back, not wanting to go too far or too fast, and possibly spoil what was beginning to be the best relationship of my life.

I knelt beside the sofa, poured wine into her glass, and placed it to her lips. When she had taken a sip, I removed it and gently placed my lips upon hers. She wrapped her arms around me, stretched seductively, and just purred like a kitten.

We continued the alternate feeding, drinking, and kissing till the second bottle was almost finished. I was becoming intoxicated, not only from wine, but with the smell, the feel, the taste of this most desirable woman. All my feelings were pushing me to make love to her. Hard, deeply passionate, and never-ending sex with her. Yet something held me back. She was so sweet and vulnerable lying there. I could never do anything to hurt her or have her lose respect for me. Whatever would become of this relationship, I wanted it to last, and I would do nothing to offend her, that might cause it to come apart.

Mary was getting drowsy, and her kisses were no longer as enthusiastic as her kisses earlier in the evening. She continued to return my kisses, but there was no passion, just sleep.

I held her hand and said gently, "It's getting late. Maybe I better be leaving?"

"No. Don't leave me. Stay here by me. I just have to rest my eyes for a few moments. When I wake, I want to see you right here beside me. Martin what took you so long to find me? It seems like I waited my whole life for you. You are the nicest and yet the sexiest man I ever met. Now hold my hand while I close my eyes."

She slowly closed her eyes, turned sideways, got comfortable, and dozed off. While holding her hand, I gazed lovingly at her. She looks so sweet and secure, sleeping there, knowing somehow, that she was safe, and that I would protect her. Wanting to undress her and take my pleasure of her, somehow knowing she would not resist, was a very tempting thought, but I kept it just a thought. I only imagined all types of sexual fantasies I could have. All I did was gently hold and caress her hand.

As she slept my thoughts changed. They went from sexual desires, to tenderness, to long lasting relationships. Pictures of us getting married, living together, having a family, and living out our lives together. During those moments, I realized that I was in love with her. Truly and deeply in love. There have been other times when I had thought I had been in love, but within a brief time those feelings passed, and I recognized that it was never love, just passion. This overwhelming feeling, I have now must be love, true love. The love of poets and novelists. The type that would make me give her everything I had and yet ask nothing in return. Just to be near her and loved in return. Looking at her, my heart overflowed with love and the strangest thing happened. Tears started to flow from my eyes and would not stop. At that moment, I solemnly pledged my undying love for her, and promised never to do her any harm. As the minutes passed, I thought was this true love? Or was it an overdose of wine and sweet passion? Looking down at Mary, I knew it was love.

CHAPTER 29

Waking slowly, I didn't know where I was. All I could remember was this beautiful dream of Martin and me, kissing and hugging. My tongue felt thick, and I had the beginning of a headache, and I had to go to the bathroom. Opening my eyes fully, I saw Martin's face close to me. Was this still a dream? Then I felt my hand in his and heard him say, "Good morning. You slept a little longer than a few minutes."

The whole wonderful evening was recalled. It wasn't a dream. My Marty was here, still here. I smiled and said, "I'm glad you're still here. I apologize for falling asleep, but I just could not keep my eyes open any longer. How long was I sleeping?"

"Only about 35 minutes. That is OK. I just held your hand and looked at you."

"Oh, I bet I look horrible and probably snored."

"No. You didn't snore, and you looked very peaceful and quite pretty. I enjoyed just sitting here with you." Then I leaned toward her and gently kissed her lips. "Good morning sweet Mary."

"The kiss was sweet, but I have to get up and go to the bathroom and pee." How could I say that? It was so crude so unladylike. Yet the way I feel with Martin, so intimate, so together, that I feel we could speak about intimate things without fear of harming our closeness.

"Let me help you up." I took her hands and gently helped her to rise. We stood facing each other, looking into each other's eyes, and fell into a passionate embrace. Our lips were locked together, and our tongues were deeply probing. The feel of her breasts and belly pressed hard against me was overwhelming. The embrace lasted for minutes. Mary slowly relaxed and slipped out of my arms and said, "I'm sorry Marty, but I just have to pee."

I tried to smile sweetly, kissed my finger, and pressed it against his adorable lips, and whispered. "Don't go away. I'll be right back."

Walking to the bath I was surprised how unsteady I was. Did it come from the wine or the kisses? After relieving myself, and rinsing my hands and face with cold water, I was still unsteady walking back to Martin. I took his hand in mine reached up and kissed his cheek and said, "Martin I'm a little drunk and I feel like lying down for a while. But not on that small sofa. Come with me."

Taking his hand, I led him to my bedroom. Falling down onto the bed, I said, "I just have to close my eyes for a few minutes, but when I wake up, I want to see you close to me. If I sleep, promise you won't leave."

"Go to sleep. I'll be right here till you wake."

She just smiled, cuddled up and contentedly fell asleep. I stood there for a minute just looking at her. More in love with her than ever. Knowing that she trusts me and believes I will take care of her.

She should be made more comfortable as she sleeps. I removed her slippers and placed them on the floor. She was wearing stockings or pantyhose under her pajama bottoms. Should I remove them also? Or just the pajama bottoms? I decided to do neither. Sliding covers from underneath her, I covered her sleeping body with just a light blanket. Looking down at her, I decided to unbutton the top button of her pajama top. Doing this I saw the swell of her breasts from beneath her bra, and unable to suppress the uncontrollable urge, I gently kissed her sweet white flesh, then feeling ashamed, yet a little thrilled, I covered her up and stepped back.

What was I to do now? I did not feel right staying here while she slept but I had said I would stay till she woke. It looks like Mary is sound asleep and will stay asleep for quite a few hours. I silently left the room and walked through her apartment. I relived myself in the bathroom and washed my hands and face. I saw my face was covered with slight traces of Mary's lipstick. Remembering all those sensual kisses, I reluctantly scrubbed them off.

Deciding to stay, I moved a chair into Mary's bedroom, into a corner, and tried to get comfortable. I decided to remove my shoes and shirt, and taking her extra pillow, curled up on her chair. Sleep did not come quickly, even if the hour was late, and I had too much wine. Just being able to glance across the room and see Mary, gave me such a feeling of contentment, that the joy I felt kept me awake. I finally dozed off in a mood of bliss and love.

CHAPTER 30

Waking to the rays of sunlight streaming through the window, I felt stiff, as if I hadn't moved during the night. My tongue felt coated and thick. While stretching, I suddenly realized I was still dressed. Looking down, I saw my lounging pajamas. I had no memory of putting them on. Slowly the events of last night returned to my memory, and a sweet, contented feeling overcame me as the particulars drifted through my mind. But not the entire evening. The latter part of the evening was blank. How did I get into bed still dressed? How did the evening end? When did Martin leave me? What did he say?

Did Martin make love to me, and I cannot remember that this morning? An event as important as losing one's virginity, and I cannot remember. I don't feel like I lost anything.

What happened to Martin? When did he leave? Did he say he would phone, or did he make another date? Darn this memory lapse. I will never drink that much again. Maybe he left a message somewhere.

Getting up slowly, I decided to look through the apartment for any kind of note. Martin would not have left me without some kind of message. Maybe he said something, and I was too drunk to remember. What a fool I was to drink so much. What does he think of me? Some kind of drunk he might not want to see again.

Thinking how nice the evening went, how romantic, how sensual, and yet filled with so much love. How did it end? Did I do or say something to spoil it? Have I lost him, after only one date? The most romantic and sensual evening of my life, and I cannot remember the ending.

Standing I started to weave toward the bath, when looking in the corner, I saw the most beautiful sight in the world. There was Martin, slouched in a chair, arms wrapped around a pillow, shoes, and shirt off. Sound asleep. Minutes seemed to pass, as I stood there just gazing at him, hardly breathing, less I woke him. My heart was racing, and I couldn't suppress a smile. He didn't leave me. We did not make love because we both are almost fully clothed, and he is not in bed with me. So, it did not happen. That is why I have no recollection of anything happening.

But why is he here? Why didn't he leave? Why is he sleeping in such an uncomfortable chair here in my bedroom? Should I wake him?

Wide awake now, I decided to make my appearance better. Quietly I went to the bath, relieved myself, then washed as silently as possible. I brushed my hair and was glad for the short curly style as it looked quite presentable this morning. I brushed my teeth, applied a little makeup and deodorant, and just a drop of cologne and stood back to look at my image. I still look rather good except my outfit was wrinkled. There was no way I could go to my closet and get a change of clothes without waking Martin.

Leaving the bathroom, I walked silently toward Martin, stopping just once to admire him again. I leaned over him and gently placed a kiss up on his cheek. When he started to move and open his eyes, I said, "Good morning, Martin. Have a nice sleep?"

He looks startled as he opened his eyes wide and glanced around the room. Then recognition appeared as he smiled sweetly and said, "Good morning, Mary."

Our heads were remarkably close and as I moved even closer, his arms enveloped me. Our lips met and what started out as a sweet romantic good morning type kiss, rapidly changed to hard, passionate, heart stopping kiss. Soon, our tongues were probing each other's mouths, bodies pressed against each other, as much as possible, in the confines of that small chair. My blood was pulsating, my body temperature rising, and a very warm ache between my thighs was causing all kinds of distraction.

The feelings throughout my body were giving me so much pleasure, I felt like I would never move. This was the best wake up ritual of my life, and parts of my mind kept saying, this is the way I should wake up every morning, in Martins embrace. I was so overwhelmed with desire and yet so deeply and thoroughly in love.

The kissing continued, deeper and more passionate. I turned and curled snugly into Martin's lap; his arm encircled me. His hand was placed on my rear and hip. Its warmth, rubbing, and squeezing was very distracting, yet very pleasurable. His other hand found my breast, hesitated, then slowly started to squeeze and caress it. That caused such a feeling of desire and wanton lust, I had never felt like this before.

My desire for Martin became so great that I threw all my restraints away. I withdrew my lips from his and whispered, "Unbutton my top." I then wrapped my arms around his neck and resumed kissing his lips with intense sensual passion.

As I felt his fingers fumbling with the buttons, I leaned backwards to give him a little more room. Soon his hand was on my bra and waves and waves of hot desire were flowing through my breast. Then his fingers were on my bare skin, then on and around my nipple. The passion, the pleasure that his touch caused was overwhelming. I was ready and willing to strip and drag him into my bed and make love to him. Never had I felt like this. This is a mix of love, passion, and uncontrollable desire.

I decided the time, the place, and the man was right. It was time to lose my virginity. My body could not wait as it was so warm and moist, so ready for its first man. I felt so ripe, my nipples so hard, I was ready to explode.

I released my lock on Martin's lips and leaned back to speak. Ready to tell him to take me. Here on the chair, on the floor, or on my bed, anyplace, but to hurry before I burst with the desire within me. "Let's stop for a moment, Martin." Before I could continue to tell him, I am yours, take me now. Make love to me. He stopped what he was doing, his hand withdrew from my bra, and his other hand relaxed on my rear. He sat up straighter and pushed me slightly away.

CHAPTER 31

Martin

Waking up from my partial sleep, all cramped and stiff, with blurred segments of dreams, both romantic and sensual, floating to my mind, all with my Mary. I felt a soft kiss upon my cheek. Opening my eyes, I saw the girl of my dreams, standing before me. Beautiful, sexy, desirable, and smiling mischievously.

The vision then spoke. "Good morning, Martin. Have a nice sleep?"

Realization slowly returned to my wine marinated brain. This is no vision. This is my Mary. I am still in her bedroom. We spent the night together. The evening memories return with those romantic events of the night. The sight of Mary caused me to smile. I said, "Good morning, Mary."

Our heads were close and as she moved closer, I reached for her, and squeezed her to me. We started to kiss in a good morning type manner. Quickly the kiss changed to a hard open mouth wet kiss, driven by passion and desire. Pulling her onto my lap she snuggled close as our lips never parted. My arms enwrapped her, my hand falling onto her sweet, sexy, soft, round bottom. My hand had a will of its own, as it started to squeeze and caress her. Each moment brought forth moans, and sighs, of pleasures. So, I continued the pleasing touch.

My other hand touched her breast and as I was about to remove it, she moved somehow into my hand and kissed my lips harder. So, my hand remained. Soon that hand had a will of its own, as it slowly caressed her breast. I could feel her hard nipple through the cloth of her top and bra and slowly and lovingly rubbed it between my fingers.

Mary withdrew her lips from mine and whispered into my ear, "Unbutton my top." She then returned to kissing me in a hard animal fashion.

I had tensed up. Thinking I had gone too far, too fast, and she was going to ask me to stop. Now I had such an overwhelming feeling of love, mixed with lust, that I had to restrain myself from ripping off her clothes and making love to her here, on the floor in her bedroom. My excitement was reaching a never before peak and my erection was hard and throbbing as it strived to rise but was held down by the weight of Mary's body.

My hand was nervous as it fumbled with the buttons. Mary leaned backwards to give me more room, while still maintaining intense pressure on my lips. Finally, the buttons were free, and my hand slid underneath her top and felt the lacy frills of her bra. Quickly my fingers were underneath and touching the smooth erotic warm flesh. When they worked their way to touch and caress her nipple, Mary let out a moan, and embraced me harder, and her tongue probed deeper into my mouth. Her nipple was hard and very large as I rubbed it between my fingers. Never had I received so much pleasure from this kind of foreplay. Removing my fingers from her nipple, I slipped her bra away and grasped her whole naked breast in my hand. I just held it, then slowly and gently squeezed. My emotions were so high I wanted to explode with desire.

Mary stopped kissing me and leaned back saying, "Let's stop for a moment."

My feelings of joy, lust, and desire suddenly froze. Had I gone too far and too fast? After all, this was still our first date. She must think that I have no respect for her. I hope I did not spoil our relationship. I removed my hand from her breast, and withdrew it from underneath her top, and stopped caressing her rear with my other hand. I struggled to sit straighter and move slightly apart.

"I'm sorry Mary. I got carried away. I went too far but my emotions took over. You're right to stop me before I did anything worse."

Mary just looked at me with a sweet smile on her face, placed both hands on my face and lovingly, yet softly, kissed me on the lips. She then hugged me and whispered into my ear, "You didn't do anything wrong. I wanted you to do what you did and enjoyed it very much. Let us just take a break and talk."

She sat further back on my lap, took both of my hands in hers and said, "Tell me what happened last night. The last thing I remember was kissing you between drinks of wine while we were on the sofa."

CHAPTER 32

“ Well, the first thing that happened, was me spilling some wine on your pretty green dress. Then you went to clean it and came back wearing this outfit. We continued kissing and drinking till you got drowsy and took a nap on the sofa for a few minutes. After insisting that I stay with you. When you woke, we started kissing again, but you were getting very sleepy and wanted to lie on your bed. You insisted I stay here so that when you woke up, you would be able to see me. So, I stayed all night. I don't think you expected to sleep all night,”

“I covered you and took off your slippers. I put you to bed and spent the rest of the night just looking at you, till I fell asleep. Nothing else happened.”

“Thank you for taking such loving care of me. It sounds like I had an enjoyable time. The parts that I remember, I know I enjoyed, but you did not have to sit up all night, cramped in that chair. You could have laid on the bed beside me and got comfortable. I was too out of it to know what you could have done.”

“No, Mary. That would not have been right, although I thought about it.” I could not tell her that I wanted to spend the night with my arms around her, holding, protecting her.

"Thank you again, for taking care of me, and especially, for staying all night so we could be together this morning." Walking close to him, I placed my palms on his cute but rough cheeks, and gently kiss his lips. Within seconds, we were engulfed in each other's arms, and kissing passionately. His arms on my back, pressing me to him. My arms around his neck, thrusting my body up and into him. The moment changed into minutes. I felt blissfully content, yet on fire with a burning passion. Everything about Martin seemed perfect. Maybe too good to be true, but he was just the right man for me. I realized I was in love with him. Deeply, eternally, completely in love, and so happy and contented, here in his arms.

I stopped kissing him and backed away. "It seems like I'm always breaking off our kisses. It does not mean I don't like them. I like them very much, as you must be able to tell by now. Let's separate for a while."

His cute face turned into a pretended frown, then he just grinned. "Okay Mary let's take a break. Not for too long. I am getting to become accustomed to having you in my arms, within kissing range. I like being able to kiss you whenever I want, and I want too always."

When I heard that, I swear my heart skipped several beats. I was so deliriously happy. I approached him and held his arms down at his sides, and gently placed a kiss upon his lips, and said, "Thank you. That was sweet to hear."

"It's after 8:00 o'clock. If you are hungry, I can fix some breakfast. I don't have a big menu, but I can scrape something together, that is, if you want to stay?"

"I want to stay, just to be near you. Although I am a little hungry, I feel that I should leave soon. I have worn these clothes too long, and I need a shave and a shower. Also, somewhere I lost my shoes. I want to look my best for you, Mary."

"Oh Martin, you look fine to me." In fact, he looked gorgeous. Standing there in his socks and wrinkled clothes. A start of a beard on his cheeks. Hair all array from my fingers, a smudge of my lipstick on his lips. He looked perfect. Just what I had always dreamt to see in my house, in the morning. "Let me fix you a little breakfast." I could not bear the thought of him leaving me now, not after last night and this morning. All those kisses, and the romance that transpired during these last few hours.

Going into the kitchen, I started to make a pot of coffee. Looking through the freezer and refrigerator, I saw my resources were at an all-time low. There was frozen orange juice and pancake mix and syrup, some milk, and two eggs left. "I hope you like pancakes, because that's all there is."

"Pancakes are fine Mary." I said, as I entered the small kitchen. I slid my arms around her and pulled her to me and started to kiss the back of her neck. "Do you need any help?"

Almost fainting from joy, I felt his arms envelope me and felt his kisses on my neck. Here in my own kitchen, in the morning, as if we were married. That was the first time marriage entered my mind. It was always there in the recesses of my thoughts. Oh, it is too early to think of that. This is still our first date, although the longest and best date ever. "No. I don't need any help. If you stay here, I'll never get anything done. Why don't you freshen up, while I prepare things?"

Hurrying up, I put last night's dirty dishes in the dishwasher, set the table and started to mix the batter. This was just like being married. There was that word again. Married. It seems to pop up into my mind often this morning.

Entering Mary's bathroom, I took my time to look around. The scents in that room reminded me of her. It was so feminine with the flowers and knickknacks. So different from my bath, which is usually decorated with dirty towels and clothes. Putting some toothpaste on my finger, I scrubbed my teeth. Then washed my face. Drying, her scent was in the towels, causing me to miss her, even though she was just in the next room. Running my fingers through my hair, I looked at myself in the mirror, and realized Mary was the girl for me. The woman I wanted to spend the rest of my life with. Get married. Yes, very good possibly. I have to get back to her.

Breakfast was spent in cordial chatter, without any kissing. The time went fast as we continued to learn more about each other. Our likes, our dreams. Clearing the table, I was as contented as I could be. Very domesticated. Taking care of my man. I put the dirty dishes in the dishwasher and turned to Martin and said, "Now what?"

"I like to see you later today. This afternoon, or evening, or both."

"That would be nice, Martin. I'm free all day."

"I have to go home first, to shower and change clothes. Then I can come back here for you."

Overflowing with joy, that he still wants to see me, I ran to him, hugged him, then started kissing him. Tears started to flow. I was so happy. Again, our kissing turned from sweetness to passion, as I ground my body to him. His hands roamed over my body. Breaking away, I smiled at him and said, "I have a better idea. Why don't you wait here while I shower and change? Then we can both go to your place. Besides, you have seen where I live, now let me see your place."

"Okay. That way we don't have to be apart." She must feel the same as I do. We are so right for each other. So natural together. I do not want to spend any time away from her.

"Good. Now you go sit on the sofa while I get ready. But what should I wear?"

"Dress casual. We'll just go to local places."

While showering, I wondered what to wear. Decided on a pair of slacks and a light blouse. I washed my hair and rubbed oil all over my skin. Thinking about Martin, the rubbing and warmth of the shower was starting to arouse me. It was hard not to call to Martin, to come here and take me. I had to turn the water to cold to get thoughts of him out of my mind. I quickly finished drying my hair. I was surprised to see how the curls were retained. I was glad I changed my hairstyle. I wrapped my naked body in my flimsy robe and went to my bedroom, hoping Martin would see and come after me. Would he like my naked body as much today as he did when I stripped for him at Rosa's?

He was sitting on the sofa looking the other way. As I dressed, I thought of numerous ways I could tell him about that night and how I became a onetime stripper, but none seemed right. I must tell him soon or never reveal a thing as long as I live.

Finishing, I hurried to him and said, "I'm ready. How do I look?"

"You look lovely, but I think you need a kiss to finish it off."

"Okay, but just one or we'll never leave."

Walking toward her as she stood there, all shiny and glowing, lips puckered, waiting for me, my heartbeat so rapidly, my knees were weak, as if I were going to meet my bride. That thought remained as I gently and sweetly just brushed my lips to hers. "Let's go."

CHAPTER 33

M y arm was around her as we walked to my car, and I squeezed her close to me. She looked very pretty and vivacious as we laughed and smiled. She looked like a young college girl today, not like the beautiful professional of the other day. To be sure, still beautiful, more so in fact, and just glowing this morning. "Your reputation will be ruined if your neighbors see you. Leaving your place with me, and it's still only mid morning."

"Who cares what they think." I hope they see this sight every morning, I giggled to myself. I then put my arm around him and hugged him. "There. Let them talk about that."

At the car he opened and held the door for me, and just before I slid into the seat, I reached up and placed a long hard kiss on his lips. "Let them talk about that too."

I drove slowly to my apartment, using just my left hand, while my right hand was being held and kissed by Mary the whole way.

"You should let me go in first. To straighten up things. I wasn't expecting company this morning."

"Is it always clean and just messy today?" Mary teased.

"I usually clean at the end of the week and just pile things up during the week. But you see, today is Saturday and it is at its worst. I don't want you to think of me as a slob."

"That's okay. I won't mind." Good. He is worried what I think so he must care what I feel toward him. I hope it is not a sty.

I parked near to my apartment and helped Mary out. We held hands as we walked up the stairs and to the door. I opened it wide and gestured with a flourish. "Home sweet home. Be it ever so humble." Repressing the feeling to lift her up into my arms and carry her across the threshold, as if she were my bride, I waved her in.

Wishing he would carry me into his home, and take me right now, anywhere, bed or floor. I slowly looked around. My first time alone in a man's home, and with the man of my dreams. Oh, my heart was pounding so fast.

His apartment was larger than mine. A large living room, nicely decorated in a college dorm style, but clean and neat, with just a trace of dust. A small den with computer and desk and books. Medium kitchen, well equipped, with just a few dishes in the sink. His bedroom showed more of his personality. Wrinkled bed but made. A hamper full, dirty clothes around it. A pair of trousers hanging on every available doorknob. Shoes lined up in a corner. His bathroom was a mess. Dirty towels on the floor, shaving equipment all over the sink, combs and brushes haphazardly lying around, and the toilet seat up. Overall, I loved it. It will not take long to train him. Besides, he was not expecting company. I thought I could make this into a very cozy first home. I felt myself blushing with that thought. This is still our first real date, although going into its second day. "It is a very nice place. I approve."

I followed Mary round like a lost puppy, as she slowly walked from one messy room to another, not saying anything. She must think I am a big slob. When she turned to me with a smile, and said she approved, I let my breath out and relaxed. I said," This was the worst day to visit."

She walked toward me, placed her arms slowly around my neck, and began kissing me. It started with warm sensual kisses but soon became hungry mouth, tongue probing, body thrusting, hot passionate kisses.

My knees were rubbery, my thighs wet, my breasts hard, and my nipples just burning for his touch. I wanted him so badly. More so than last night or this morning. A very small part of my brain said stop. Damn that part. Didn't Dolly and Janet always say, sex on the first date ruins everything. The man will always treat me you like a tramp.

Pulling our lips apart and taking a deep breath, I said, "I'm enjoying this. Enjoying it very much, as you can tell. Let's cool it a little. Please."

"Mary, I'm enjoying this too. I want you so badly I can hardly control myself. I can't just get enough of your kisses, your mouth. the touch of your breasts. and the feel of your body. I never have felt like this. If I did not feel like I do, we would both be naked on the floor and making love. It is very difficult for me to cool it right now."

His words made me weak all over. I sagged against his heaving chest. A great warmth flashed through me. He said he felt toward me as I felt toward him. I pushed myself a few inches away, took a deep breath and said, "You said you felt toward me. How do you feel toward me?"

"Mary, my Mary. I can't keep you out of my mind. I can't keep my hands off of you. I can't bear to be apart from you. I want you near me always. I have a tough time breathing when you're near me, and my heart has a hard time beating when we're apart."

I was going to say that I felt the same, but it was just too soon to tell him that. Later, but not too far in the future. "Martin, I don't know how I feel. I have never felt like this before. I have never acted like this before. I like what we are doing. Everything is happening so fast, that I cannot express how I feel. I am very confused but incredibly happy to be with you." I reached up and placed a warm kiss upon his lips, then withdrew from his arms.

CHAPTER 34

66 Just sit down and make yourself comfortable, while I take a shower and change. I won't be long." I mumbled, as I picked a change of clothes and underwear and tried to enter the bathroom while trying to cover my body with clothing. I was glad I took the time to buy those new pairs. It would be a horrible time to be without clean underwear.

He looks so flustered as he left the room, as if he weren't used to having company at such an intimate moment. That is good. It means that he hadn't had girls staying overnight before, I think. The quick look I had of his jockey shorts gave me a strange feeling, not sexual, but more intimate. As if we were familiar. One day I could be doing his laundry, and then we would be a family.

While he showered, I examined the apartment in detail. I didn't go through any drawers, although I was tempted, just looked at every object. As if they could tell me more about him. His books were on a whole variety of subjects, mystery, sports, and history. A wide range of sport equipment, for various sports, were lying in corners, all used and slightly dirty. His stereo and CD player were decent quality but his taste in music was different than mine. His small collection of music was all of the oldies, and a few classics. Not like my collection of show music and operettas. There were pictures of sports teams and I recognized Martin and his three friends in them. The other photos were of family, I think. They resemble Martin. One photo that bothered me, was of a lovely young girl, very pretty. Was she an old girlfriend or a relative? I will have to ask him about her.

Overall, his apartment pleased me. It was what I expected to find. Although it was my first time in a man's apartment. It just needed a good cleaning and a little rearranging. I could fix this place up real cozy. I started daydreaming about moving in and sharing everything, but after looking in the closets, I knew there wasn't room for my things. We will just have to find a bigger place for the two of us. I smiled as I thought of us in the future.

I no longer heard the water running, so I tapped on the door, and said, "What's taking you long? Can I come in?" Never would I have said that to anyone, especially a man, in my whole life. That is, before I met Martin. My whole personality was changing since I met him. I was becoming a brazen flirt and it felt good. Knocking again, I said, "If you don't come out now, I'm coming in."

Hurrying through the shower, I dried myself and started to shave, when I heard Mary knock. Standing there naked I almost opened the door for her but thought better of it. Believing it just to be a joke, I said nothing and finished my shave. The thought of Mary, here in my bathroom, while I was naked, aroused me so much, that I had to step away and calm myself, or else I could cut my throat. I quickly donned my underwear, trousers, and socks. I was applying deodorant when she knocked again, and I heard, "If you don't come out now, I'm coming in." My desire for her overwhelmed my inhibitions and I opened the door and said, "Come in, if you must."

Much to my surprise the door opened, and Martin standing there, nude from the waist up, with wisps of steam swirling around him. It was such a marvelous sight that my knees almost buckled. He was the man of my dreams. The man I waited for. My future. With a gasp, I ran into room and flung my arms around him, saying, "I missed you so much. I couldn't wait." With all abandonment gone, I kissed his chest, neck, cheeks, and lips. I thrusted my eager body against him, letting him know I was ready and willing for anything.

When I opened the door Mary was standing there with a sad but sweet smile, saying, "I missed you so much. I couldn't wait." My heart swelled to near bursting with love and longing, but before I could move or say anything, Mary was in my arms kissing my check, neck, and lips. My arms enfolded her as I pulled her closer. The swell of her breasts against my bare chest, the pressure of her belly against my lower body, the slow undulations she was making, and the pressure of her lips on mine, with the added thrill of our tongues playing together, was causing a major erection. If I did not stop soon, I would ejaculate and ruin this moment. Pulling my lips away, I whispered, "Mary please back away. I cannot stand this desire anymore. Either we have to make love, right now, here on my bed or we just have to keep apart for a while."

Releasing my grip on his shoulders, and just playfully running my hands across this bare chest, I dreamily looked up into his eyes and said, "I want what you want."

"I don't know what I want. I want you very badly. I also do not want to spoil something that has become very special to me. Having sex with a girl changes everything. Especially early in a relationship. I'm sorry to say this but before we met, I had relations with girls that I thought I liked, but all changed after having sex with them. Our relationships became sordid and soon broke apart. I don't think that will happen to us. I am not willing to take a chance of losing you. I am going to hate myself later for saying this. Let's wait till we know each other better and know for sure that the time is right."

My heart was bursting with love for this man. He wants me yet doesn't want to spoil this glorious relationship. I love him so much that my entire body aches for his touch. It is he, that I saved myself for. I know that now and I am willing to do anything for him or to him. Is he right? I think so. All my friends say the relationship changes after having sex, and soon it breaks apart. The only girls I know that have a long term sexual relationship with a man are either married or went with the man a while before having sex. Better to not take chances, even though the wetness between my legs, is trying to convince me to say, let's have sex now.

"As long as I know you want me, and you know I want you. Sometimes soon it is going to happen. I can wait." I backed away from him and playfully curled his chest hairs around my fingers "I'll leave you now. Don't take too long. I'll go sit on that sofa, like a good little girl."

I was regretting letting Mary leave me for my desire was enormous. Yeah, I knew we did the right thing. Did not let passion ruin what is becoming a beautiful relationship. If my dreams workout, there will be many occasions in the near future for sex, and may they never end.

Finishing my absolutions, I went to my bedroom and finished dressing. I dressed like Mary, wearing slacks and my best clean shirt. Every time I glanced in the other room; Mary was sitting there. Primly with a sweet smile. Wouldn't it be nice if this could happen every day? My Mary, here with me. Near me. Living with me.

When I finished dressing, I want to Mary, held out my hands to her and brought her into my arms. Holding her firmly yet gently, I placed a slow gentle kiss upon her lips, breaking away before anything started. I said, "Let's leave before I change my mind."

CHAPTER 35

As I helped Mary into the car, I wondered where to go. Someplace with a lot of people so that I would be forced to keep my hands off her. Not too public, so that I could still touch and hold her. "Mary, have you ever been to the zoo?"

"No. I've never have been there but always wanted to go. It just seemed that I never had the time. I would like to go today."

I reached across the console and touched his hand. The feeling of contentment that it gave me was so sweet, so right, so perfect, that I hesitated to let it go, when he needed both hands to negotiate a turn. I sat sideways the whole trip and just glanced at him and blissfully dreamed of our future together. Yes, there will be a future together. I am sure of it.

We parked and took the escalator ride to the top of the hill. Holding hands, we joined in with the happy and playful children.

At the children's zoo I stood back and just watched Mary pet and hug all the little furry animals, even the tiger cubs. She seemed to fit right in with the children as she cavorted with and petted the felines. Every time she picked up a kitten and hugged it, she would look at me with a big smile and blew kisses at me. She had to feed and pet every animal there.

This day was continuing to be a special day in my life. As we strolled past the exhibits, holding hands, and hugging every time we stopped at a different animal section. Martin would kiss me gently on the cheek or neck. In the underground section it was chilly, so Martin had to hold me close, remarkably close during the entire trip. That was the dreamy part of the visit that I will never forget.

As we walked along a path around the outdoor cagelesss enclosures, that the big animals were kept, all in the bright sun, I worried about Mary. She seemed to be walking with a limp. "Are you okay?"

"I'm fine. It just that my shoes are a little tight, and walking these hills is a problem. I'll be fine. Let's keep going."

"We saw most of the zoo and besides, I'm getting hungry. Let's leave and go to lunch."

I was glad to leave for I had dressed for style, not for walking. I would never have mentioned my sore feet. It was a grand day so far. "Alright Marty. I've had enough today but I like to come back again and see the rest."

As we settled back into my car, Mary looked flushed and tired. The day was hot and humid, and the long walk had worn her out. I have to take her to a nice cool spot for lunch. "Let us eat lunch on the Allegheny River. I know a nice cool place to eat and relax"

"Okay. Anything you say." It was a nice feeling, to let everything up to Martin. To be taken care of and protected, like being a part of a family. I leaned my head back and just held Martin's hand and enjoyed the ride.

Driving to the barge on the river, we passed Rosa's nightspot. That caused me to think about the Dancer again. It seemed like weeks since the last time I thought about her. Ever since I met Mary, she was the only girl on my thoughts now. My mind reviewed that night again, as I had done hundreds of times before. Just the thought of her was causing a slight erection. I glanced at Mary leaning back with her eyes closed slightly. I realized that she could not see my aroused state. Odd, I never noticed it before but there was a resemblance between Mary and the Dancer. Both about the same size and height, but the Dancer was much more voluptuous, and older. The Dancer had longer and darker hair, and a fuller and darker face. Her breasts were much larger than Mary's, even though I had only felt Mary's, they seem smaller. Another thing, Mary was always smiling while the Dancer never smiled, and somehow seemed sad. There was just a superficial resemblance. Maybe it is just that I am attracted to a certain type of female. I best get that woman, that whore out of my mind, and never ever mention her to Mary.

As the car slowed, I roused myself from my sweet dreams and glance sideways and saw Rosa's. We were not going to go there, were we? My nerves cooled somewhat as Marty passed Rosa's without a word and turned into a parking lot near the river. It is still too soon since that foolish day when I made such an ass of myself. That ruse would never have worked on Martin. We could never have become what we are today, if we had talked that day, as planned with those fools, Dolly and Janet. I look different now. My hair is lighter, cut short and curled. Not like the long straight dark hair I had that horrible night. I am glad the girls made me wear of lot of that dark makeup.

He cannot recognize me as that stripper, not now. After we met ideally, and he likes me as I am. For what I am. Maybe it was luck that we did not make love last night. Could my naked body on my bed cause Martin to remember my naked body that night? I better defer having sex with Martin until our relationship is on good healthy normal grounds. If he has any memories of that other night, they will be forgotten soon. I just pray he never remembers.

For a hot sunny day, the restaurant was ideal. The breeze from the river cooled me. The atmosphere was fresh, yet romantic. Just what I needed. I ordered iced tea. No more alcohol for me, not for a long while. I have no defenses to resist Martin when sober and with a few drinks I know I couldn't resist him again tonight. Not that I resisted him much last night. I am so glad that Martin respected me enough to not take advantage of me. Even if I was asking him, not so many words, to make love to me. He is so sweet I just could not resist. I leaned toward him and placed a long wet kiss on his cheek. "Thanks."

"What was that for? Not that I minded."

"I just had to kiss you, here and now."

We had a slow yet romantic lunch that lasted most of the afternoon. We chatted all the time, mostly Mary talking and I listening. Never had I spent time with a girl that I could talk to, like being with Mary. Even when I am with my male friends, conversation didn't flow so smoothly. There were no embarrassing pauses when a lull occurred. It was just a good feeling to be in each other's company. This has to be the girl of my dreams. My future lifelong companion. My wife.

Early evening fell as we left, and I felt a slight panic. What are we to do the rest of the evening? I know if Martin takes me back to my place this early, I will have him in my bed within an hour. Never mind how delicious the thought was, I didn't want that to happen tonight. Soon. very soon, but not tonight. Tonight, I just could not refuse him, and I do not want him to know that.

Walking from the barge, I had my arm around Mary, and she was pressed against me. Each step we took, although a little awkward was very unusual. As her right leg, thigh, and hip, moved in step with my left leg, thigh, and hip we laughed and hugged all the way to my car. She was the nicest, pleasantness and sexiest girl I had ever been with. The girl who I was searching for, all my life.

After buckling myself in, I said, "What are our plans now."

"I don't want this day to end. It has been good. Where do you like to go? To see a movie or we could rent a video?"

Spending a nice evening watching a video, curled up with Martin, sounds good. Too good. "A movie sounds good. Why don't you select one?"

I bought a paper, and we selected a current movie at a mall, only a short drive away. The movie wasn't crowded, and we sat off by ourselves. I spend half the time watching the screen and the rest watching Mary, as she clutched my hand during the surprise scenes or cried during the sad parts. My heart nearly burst with love for this sweet girl. I could never do anything to hurt her or even let harm come to her. I silently pledged to honor and protect her for the rest of my life.

The movie ended happily, and I wiped away my tears with Martin's hanky. "I'm glad you selected this movie. I always cry during a sad part and also during happy endings. Why don't we just go home. My makeup is spoiled, and I am not hungry. If that's all right with you?"

"That's fine Mary. It's been a long day. A very pleasant day. You must be tired."

When we got to my apartment, Martin walked me to the door and was very gentle as he kissed me in the hall. All my resolve was gone, and I could not let him say goodnight. "Come in for a few minutes, please. I don't feel like kissing you here in the hall."

Taking his hand, I pulled him in inside, although he was not resisting. Inside, I closed the door and put my arms around him and kissed him in the sexiest most wanton manner I could think of. I pressed myself against him and ground my hips and breast against his body for minutes, then gently pulled myself away.

"Thanks for a perfectly lovely day, Martin. I enjoyed myself and enjoyed being with you, but you better leave now while I'm still able to let you leave."

Those kisses Mary gave me just inside her door, were the sexiest most arousing kisses of my life. I could hardly catch my breath and I was embarrassed at the erection I had. Good thing the room was dimly lit. "Before I leave, and I will leave, although I don't want to, when will I see you again?"

"Tomorrow is only Sunday. Why don't we do something in the afternoon?"

"That's my problem Mary. I want to be with you tomorrow and every day, but I promised my Mother I would spend the day with her."

My disappointment faded, as he said the only reason to be away for me was to be with his mother. I said, "That's alright, maybe next week." I then kissed his cheek and brushed back his hair.

"I have a thought. Why don't you come with me? My Mother won't mind. You will like her, and I am sure she will like you. We will just spend the afternoon, have a bite to eat and then leave. Please say you'll come."

The thought of meeting his parents scared me and yet gave me a warm feeling. Meeting a boy's parents was a step. A major step on the road to matrimony. Is this what he wants? This soon? That would be only the fifth day we would be together.

"Do you often ask girls you just met to meet your parents?"

"No. You're the first, the only girl I ever asked. It seems like we have been together a lot longer than four days."

"Asking a girl to meet a boy's parents implies serious intentions on the boy's part. If the girl accepts, it implies serious intentions on the girl's part. We have just gotten to know each other. Are there serious intentions on the boy's part?" I could not breathe, and my heart stopped beating as I waited for Martin's answer.

"Maybe it is a little early in our relationship but there are serious intentions on the boys part."

My heart started to beat again and as I took a deep breath, I flung myself into Martin's arms. Hugging and kissing him shamelessly. Martin pulled my arms down and pushed me away. I almost felt like crying.

"You didn't say you would go or not go. Are there serious intentions on the girls part?"

"Yes, I'll go with you, if you really want me to go?"

"Yes, I really want you to go with me. Now the other question. Are there serious intentions on the girls part?"

I flung myself at him, wrapped my arms around him, and said, "Couldn't you tell? Yes, the girl has serious intentions."

I kissed Mary and swung her around the room. Putting her down, I whispered, "I would have died of remorse if you had said you had no serious intentions."

"You better kiss me, then leave, or I won't let you leave it all."

I will come by for you about 2:00 PM. Nobody dresses up at our place. Just dress as you did today. I will call you before I come over. Bye."

"Bye. Till tomorrow."

CHAPTER 36

Martin

Driving home after leaving Mary, my mind was a swirl of pleasant thoughts. First, Mary feels toward me as I feel toward her. What I feel must be love. I have never felt like this before, and Mary must feel likewise. Could she love me too? Second, Mary agreed to go with me to meet my family. That might not mean anything but politeness, but it could mean she is serious about us. I know we both mentioned serious intentions. Was that just said in the heat of passion? Would Mary still feel the same way tomorrow? Third, the way I feel about Mary is very serious. I can daydream about being together, living in her own home and having a family.

Then I thought about my mother. Would she be willing to accept a guest, a female guest, on such short notice? What short notice? She doesn't even know yet. I must call her tonight. Ask permission to bring Mary. Ask if she has enough food. Ask who else will be there and many more questions that were flying through my mind. The worst thought was, what if she said no? No, Mom would never say such a thing. To such an important event. Bringing a girl home to meet her.

I did not call as soon as I got home. I paced the floor trying to calm my nerves and preparing answers to a slew of yet unasked questions. Taking a deep breath, I dialed.

"Hello"

"Hello. Mom it's me Marty"

"Is something wrong? Calling at such a late hour. You never call this late. Aren't you coming tomorrow?"

"Yes, I'm coming tomorrow. That's why I called. Would it put you out to much if I brought a friend for dinner?"

"That's no problem. You know you can always bring along one of your friends. Is it one of your college friends? Do I know him?"

"That's why I called. It is none of my friends. It is a girl, and no, you don't know her. She is from Pittsburgh."

"Sure, you can bring her with you. Is she just a friend or is this someone special? Someone you're serious about?"

"I haven't known her for too long, but she is a friend. Someone special, very special. I am serious about her and the longer I know her the more serious I get. It would mean a lot to me if you two can like each other."

"You bring your girl tomorrow and I'm sure we all will like her. There will be just your dad and Susan and Jimmy are coming this weekend. The whole family. Is there something special I should make for dinner? Does she have a special diet?"

"I don't think so. She eats about anything when we go out. Just make what you were planning. Nothing special, although you could make a pie for me."

"I'll take care of everything. Do not worry. Bring her here before dinner to give us enough time to meet and socialize."

"I'll be there around 3:00 o'clock and thanks, Mom.

"I'll see you both tomorrow. Drive carefully. Bye."

"Bye, Mom."

CHAPTER 37

Icried when Marty left. I almost opened the door and ran after him. It is strange being so happy because he has serious intentions for me, and so sad because he isn't here in my arms. If he had stayed any longer, I would have insisted we have sex. Right now, and hopefully all night. I wanted him so bad my whole body ached for him. What was happening to me? Is this how love feels"

What if his mother doesn't like me? Will it change his feelings for me? The tears started and they would not stop. Should I plead sick and not go. No, not after he made plans. Should I take a gift or some food? What does a girl take to her potential mother-in-law? My knees felt weak when I said that word. That meant marriage and family.

Not knowing what was for dinner, I decided bringing any type of food was not right. Flowers would not be appropriate. Maybe just a potted plant. A small tea rose if I can find one tomorrow morning.

Martin said dress casual, just like today. I can't wear jeans the first time I meet his family, hopefully the first of many. Looking through my closet I decided on a full skirt and a flowered blouse. Nothing sexy and a lot of my arms and legs covered.

CHAPTER 38

Martin

Sunday morning was passing slowly as I idled in my apartment. Time seemed to drag while I was waiting to see my Mary. Yes, she was already MY MARY in my mind. Thoughts and dreams with her and about her occupied my mind. I had a difficult time waiting to see her. My arms wanted to hold her, and my lips wished to kiss her.

I decided to leave early, to spend more time, more alone time with her. We have to decide how to introduce Mary. Friend? Girlfriend? Steady Girlfriend? Future Wife? No, that is too early to say that. One day soon?

Today was not the day to take some of my dirty laundry to my mom. Not in front of Mary. What would she think of me then? Still a momma's boy? No. No. Never again. I will do it all by myself from now on.

Standing in front of Mary's door, I waited and thought, this could be one of the most important days of my life.

CHAPTER 39

Stopping what I was doing when the doorbell rang, I ran to the door and flew into the arms of the man standing there. "Marty, I've missed you." We hugged and kissed for a time before I realized that we were still in the hall. Releasing myself, I said, "Come inside and sit down. You are early, I like that. It will only take me a few minutes."

"I couldn't wait. I missed you so very much."

"Now sit down beside me, we have something to talk about. It has been bothering me all morning

Mary sat near him on the sofa, a scared look upon her face. "What do we have to talk about?"

My stomach was acting up and a chill swept over myself.

"When we get to my mom's, what do I call you?"

I relaxed and my heart started beating again. Why, just call me Mary. Mary Burns."

"Not that. How do I introduce you?"

"This is my friend?

"That would be okay."

"No. Not right. This is my girlfriend?

"That sounds nice, Martin."

"No. Not right either. How is this: Here is my steady girlfriend

"That is awfully nice? But we have only been together for five days. That is a brief time to be called steady." My heart was beating rapidly, and I could hardly breath. Why was he asking these questions?

"What if I introduced you as my fiancée?

"Do you know what that means?"

"Of course, I do."

"It means that Someone has to ask Somebody a question. Then if Somebody agrees, Someone has to seal the agreement with a token. Usually a ring. None of that has happened."

"I know that."

"We have only known each other for five days." I will not count being a Dancer at Rosa's a few weeks ago.

"I know that. I have known you long enough. I know all I want or need to know."

I leaned into his arms and passionately kissed him on the lips. "Martin, before Somebody could answer Someone's question, some time would have to pass. She would have to meet the boy's family."

"Good. That will be today."

"Then the boy would have to meet the girl's family"

"Anytime. Soon."

"Then if the girl is asked properly, and if she answered in the affirmative and the symbolic token was passed, then you could use that name, none of that has happened."

Martin got off the sofa, knelt in front of Mary, and asked, "If Somebody was asked, what would she answer?"

With tears of happiness running from my eyes, I wrapped my arms him and cried happily. "What do you think?

After a few minutes of hugging and kissing, we separated. Holding her tightly, Martin said, "I'll just have to say, Girlfriend. I'll change that soon."

"Tomorrow, I'll call my parents and tell them I'm coming for a visit and that I am bring a boyfriend to meet them. We will try to make it soon."

"Then the answer to the question to the girl was?"

"After the meetings, and a little time passes, and everything is proper, then the answer is yes."

We kissed and sweetly hugged for minutes. Martin broke away and said, "Let's get started and meet my parents. We have a future to start together."

Laughing and holding hands, we walked to the car and into a blissful life.

The Beginning

CPSIA information can be obtained
at www.ICGtesting.com
Printed in the USA
LVHW081455280422
716807LV00003B/6